Hope Through Cancer

A Survivor's Journey of Hope, With an Artist's Perception, In the light of Psalm 23.

By Claude Jacques (Author and Artist)
Faith Copeland Jacques (Co-author)
Toni Williams (Assistant Editor)

Hope through Cancer

Scripture quotations from The Authorized (King James) Version. Rights in the Authorized Version in the United Kingdom are vested in the Crown. Reproduced by permission of the Crown's Patentee, Cambridge University Press.

Hope Through Cancer Publications
2012 S Federal Hwy F-207
Boynton Beach, Fl. 33435

4

P. 134   What does it mean,

"I will cross that bridge when

I get there"

Table Of Contents

Dedication

This book is dedicated to my wife for the courageous battle she is fighting, the insight she gave to understanding survivors, and her patience in helping to prepare this book.

A Survivor's Journey of Hope, With an Artist's Perception, In the light of Psalm 23.
By Claude Jacques (Artist)
Faith Copeland Jacques (Co-author)

Introduction

Cancer was the inspiration for this whole project. Eighteen months into our marriage, we faced a different journey than expected. Little did I know seven years ago, that today I would be expressing my thoughts and feelings about a journey with cancer. Our desire is to encourage others to find hope in their lives for the voyage ahead. Life has its ups and downs, but cancer does not have to be the lowest situation. Not many people can relate to what we feel, perceive, or even fear, unless they are on the same journey.

After probably experiencing denial about the possible reality of my health, my husband and I embarked on a journey with cancer the day the doctor walked down the hospital halls. In his scrubs, he came to update Claude on the extensive operation I just went through. The doctor's facial expressions announced bad news. He was faced with a difficult task of informing the whole family of the cold facts of reality they had to encounter. He explained in his best professional manner and courtesy the procedures of removing the stomach apron, a complete hysterectomy, re-section of the bowels, and more, concluding that I had stage 3C ovarian cancer. The youngest child asked if that meant it was terminal. No definite answer was given, other

than the possibility of prolonging life through chemotherapy. Time flew by quickly.

As Claude (my husband) was pondering the situation, he
found himself, down the hall, away from the adult children.
He started crying inside, visible from his shoulders moving
uncontrollably. A nurse tried to console him saying she
overheard the doctor and that she was sorry and hoped things
would work out. From that point on, we were on a path we
had never experienced or even thought we would face. Claude
wanted to be the best support ever so that I would find peace
and encouragement somehow, somewhere.

His experiential faith in God would prove to be useful. He
believed God and His promises. He believed God was in full
control of something that seemed completely out of control.
Together we faced mortality. How were we going to prepare
ourselves for the inevitable? Yes, we had our moments of tears
and sobs. My heart would break when I perceived the situation
as a death sentence. I can tell you now, our time of peace and
encouragement came from God to whom we turned to for help
and direction. He spoke to our hearts every day as we meditated on His Word and prayed. We felt God's presence in a
very remarkable way. If we were not on a journey with cancer,
we would not have experienced those precious moments that
count for so much in this world of darkness, gloom, and
sadness. There is hope through cancer.

We believed that God could do the impossible and He
would give us grace and encouragement. On this journey, we
have found opportunities of peace and support. Our loved ones
did their best to ease the pain, but only the One in control of
our circumstances could give peace like no other. It has now
been seven years, and we have experienced many different

situations. We have learned to place our confidence in the Lord who is in control of our lives.

Two months after my first operation, I had a bowel obstruction that required a return stay at the hospital for a couple of weeks. I again, underwent a serious operation. Three years from my first diagnosis, I had to go through chemo for the third time around, losing my hair and my health, (the consequences of chemotherapy). I am considered chronic because the cancer came back.

Our greatest consolation and strength are the special times together in the morning, having coffee and just talking. Since we meditate on the Bible and have daily devotions, we always seem to speak about that which lies ahead of us. We talk about what we are going through, and how God directs, strengthens and how good He is to us. There are so many instances where we see the hand of God. He is present every day, and we believe it. As we overlook the gardens from where we sit, we appreciate the beautiful trees, flowers, and grass. We are like Adam and Eve meeting God in the garden. The moments are precious. I thank God for my husband who has been a spiritual mentor and encouragement by my side. All of this inspired us to want to reach out and help others to find the same peace and support while facing cancer.

An inspiring thought came to us about the possibility of creating a beautiful oil painting that would portray a journey of peace and the penetrating light of encouragement that comes from above. Thus, the "Hope Through Cancer" oil painting started. We then embarked on an art venture. Claude thought this would be a great project for retirement, about three years away, but he was inspired to start the monumental task right away. He read and familiarized himself with artwork till he felt ready to start. He followed through by taking art classes from professionals. We entitled it, "Hope Through Cancer" because it seemed to sum up, our experience and that of everyone else going through cancer. We gave "hope" an acronym: **H**ope, **O**pportunities, **P**eace, and **E**ncouragement. Our desire for those that receive a print of the oil painting and the book that explains it, is that they find hope. In the picture, their journey begins as they go through the gate entrance, specially designed for each individual facing mortality and in need of peace and encouragement. I wanted the painting to depict tranquility, hope and help from above. Though my husband does not personally have cancer, together we have lived through it. Consequently, we want to be helpful through prayers, answering questions, and giving support in any way possible. He was inspired because I was diagnosed with the disease. Our desire is that others will also be inspired to reach out and touch others that they may find the peace that God promises and, therefore, be prepared for the days ahead. We need hope that a cure or remission be close at hand.

A picture is worth a thousand words. Giving a print of this painting to someone will mean a lot to them, just knowing that together we are on the same path. We know how they feel. All prints will be numbered and signed by the two of us as long as God allows us to be here on earth. The revenue from this painting will go towards the "Hope Through Cancer" ministries. My husband dedicated the art and this book to me.

As we look at the painting, a detailed explanation will be provided for each significant item in the artwork. Hopefully, as this picture is displayed in your home, you will remember the thoughts and meanings portrayed in our journey. On the next page you will see the oil painting that we visualized and the reasoning behind it.

We will look at it in the light of Psalm 23 which says:

1 *The LORD is my shepherd; I shall not want.*
2 *He maketh me to lie down in green pastures: he leadeth me beside the still waters.*
3 *He restoreth my soul: he leadeth me in the paths of righteousness for his name's sake.*
4 *Yea, though I walk through the valley of the shadow of death, I will fear no evil: for thou art with me; thy rod and thy staff they comfort me.*
5 *Thou preparest a table before me in the presence of mine enemies: thou anointest my head with oil; my cup runneth over.*
6 *Surely goodness and mercy shall follow me all the days of my life: and I will dwell in the house of the LORD for ever.*

Chapter 1
"The Rose."

Born and raised in a Christian home, I became a Christian, at age ten. I knew a lot about God, but I did not know God. My father had an extraordinary faith, and knew that God was real. God was very evident in his life, and that was something I always longed to have.

I wanted to be saved from hell, but I did not desire to give God control of my life. I messed up so many times, and then resented God for the mess I had made. I wanted to have God and the world, and was seeking the truth.

God was working in my life all along, even though I was not aware of it. He brought my husband Claude into my life. His faith motivated me to seek the peace and confidence that God is in control and only wants the best for me. I started praying, asking God to make Himself known to me, and He did. This experience changed my life and I felt the need to let everyone know how God can work in such marvelous ways.

In March of 2009, I was diagnosed with stage 3 ovarian cancer. God immediately gave me an indescribable peace I had never experienced. My relationship with God was just beginning. In the next couple of months, I would learn more about God than I had in the 57 years before. He has walked with me every step of this journey. I believe He has allowed this suffering in my life to help me learn to trust Him more each day and to feel His presence. Together, Claude and I have walked and grown in the Christian faith because of this journey. No matter how terrible things may seem I must remember that God has a perfect plan for me.

God's Love

In the painting as one enters the new journey, there is the red rose to welcome you, strategically placed on the gate. It reminded me of God's love, God's presence, His peace and His purpose for me. Maybe the next time I see a rose, it will remind me of God's love towards me. What will you remember the next time you see one? Life will never be the same; it will be so much better! Although, I had the love and support of my husband and family, there were times when I struggled with loneliness and helplessness. There was still a void. Fears crept up from every side. I still needed support. Where could I find it?

The greatest disaster was upon me, but the best outcome was to learn and know the love of God. At times when all is going well, we do not even think about love from the Supreme Being. If family is doing well, finances are permitting a comfortable lifestyle, plenty of friends to love, and receive love, why go beyond all of this? If work is fulfilling, allowing our essential needs for fun and life, why look for more and think of God?

The reason is very evident. There is no complete, purposeful life, without God. We are created in a way that we need a spiritual satisfaction, and this joy comes from God. In the Bible and as we look around, God's love is revealed to us through nature. **"God is love"** *is written upon every opening bud, upon every spire of springing grass. The lovely birds making the air vocal with their happy songs, the delicately tinted flowers in their perfection perfuming the air, the lofty trees of the forest with their rich foliage of living green -- all testify to the tender, fatherly care of our God and His desire to make His children happy.[1]*

I believe that our short time here on earth is to learn and discover what this love means and to what level. Though it is as complicated to us as the spiritual world itself, we can be aware of God's love in many ways. We know that there is no one on earth that has come to a complete understanding of His love, because it is beyond us to be able to comprehend the magnitude of its implication. The Bible says in Ephesians 3:18-19; *May be able to comprehend with all saints what is the breadth, and length, and depth, and height; And to know the love of Christ, which passeth knowledge, that ye might be filled with all the fulness of God.*

The living God wants to communicate with His creation. He can touch our souls and minds enabling us to face the most daunting situations in our lives. It took cancer for me to recognize that God has always been in my life and through this experience realize His precious love to me.

---

[1] (E. White)

The rose on the gate is the artist's perception of that love. A rose says so much by itself. Deep feeling is portrayed, when a man presents a rose to the one he loves, or a rose is laid on a casket of a dear one.

Red roses, as we think of them today, are the traditional symbol of love and romance. The modern red rose we are now familiar with was introduced to Europe from China in the 1800's. However, the meanings associated with them can be traced back many centuries, even to some of the earliest societies. The color red itself evolved from an old primal symbol for life into a metaphor for deep emotion. In Greek and Roman mythology, the red rose was closely tied to the goddess of love. Many early cultures used red roses to decorate marriage ceremonies, and they were often a part of traditional wedding attire. Through this practice, the red rose became known as a symbol of love and fidelity. As the tradition of exchanging roses and other flowers as gifts of affection came into prevalence, the red rose naturally became the flower of choice for sending the strongest message of love. This is a tradition that has endured to the present day.[2]

Family Love

The rose, and the love it represents, encompasses God's love and also the love of those that surrounded me. I believe anyone going through cancer who does not receive or feel love is to be greatly pitied. I want to show others that they are loved. I would like to be used by God to share His love with others, so they, too, can be blessed. My husband wanted to show his love in every way he could. He would have felt guilty if simply continuing his lifestyle, not making my situa-

[2] (Proflowers)

tion an important part of his life. Just how profound does this go? Fortunately, my husband is a giver. He struggles more with receiving than giving. Sacrifices were made, and he proved his love when many might have walked away with an insensitive heart.

I often wondered what my children felt when they saw their mother going through sickness, weakness, nausea, and pain. I think events inspire love. I appreciate the love that my family has expressed.

Even their lives are different because of my cancer. Some struggle with expressing feelings or try to hide them, but one thing is sure, their love has matured and blossomed. They have found themselves in a situation they did not desire. It changed them forever. Cancer has developed stepping stones toward compassionate hearts in all of us. What happened to me, also happened to them. They are caregivers from the outside; my husband is a caregiver from the inside, both in different ways. He continues to work and provide, not knowing my final outcome. Recently we spoke about his feelings and fears. He did not want to discuss matters too far in the future. He deals with problems and concerns by taking them as they come, on a daily basis.

The Bible teaches us in Matthew 6:26-34:

25 Therefore I say unto you, Take no thought for your life, what ye shall eat, or what ye shall drink; nor yet for your body, what ye shall put on. Is not the life more than meat, and the body than raiment?

26 Behold the fowls of the air: for they sow not, neither do they reap, nor gather into barns; yet your heavenly Father feedeth them. Are ye not much better than they?

²⁷ Which of you by taking thought can add one cubit unto his stature?

²⁸ And why take ye thought for raiment? Consider the lilies of the field, how they grow; they toil not, neither do they spin:

²⁹ And yet I say unto you, That even Solomon in all his glory was not arrayed like one of these.

³⁰ Wherefore, if God so clothe the grass of the field, which to day is, and to morrow is cast into the oven, [shall he] not much more [clothe] you, O ye of little faith?

³¹ Therefore take no thought, saying, What shall we eat? or, What shall we drink? or, Wherewithal shall we be clothed?

³² (For after all these things do the Gentiles seek:) for your heavenly Father knoweth that ye have need of all these things.

³³ But seek ye first the kingdom of God, and his righteousness; and all these things shall be added unto you.

³⁴ Take, therefore, no thought for the morrow: for the morrow shall take thought for the things of itself. Sufficient unto the day [is] the evil thereof.

His fears are subdued by putting off the inevitable until the time when it becomes real. He is concerned about being weak and not having the faith to overcome the trial that could be ahead of him. So together, we encourage each other in our faith. We want to grow in God's love and be found faithful to Him to the end.

I like what Dennis J. De Haan said in one of his meditations; *I had never thought of worry as a form of taking on God's responsibility. But the more I thought about it, the more I realized that worry, in its naked form, comes close to doing just that. I thought of this after seeing a sign in a church foyer that read:*

Do not feel totally, personally, irrevocably responsible for everything. That is My job. —God

This advice does not absolve us of all responsibility, however. The force of the statement lies in the words totally, personally, irrevocably, and everything. We often feel we must solve all our problems ourselves, and that unless we come up with the right solution all will be lost. Only God has sufficient energy and wisdom to handle everything well. Worry will gradually lose its hold on our lives if we learn to stop playing God[3].

Our God loves us enough to take care of us and to manifest his love to us. Everything around us reminds us of the love He has for His own and those that seek Him. To have a relationship with Him is to know Him personally and to love others. It can be very difficult for us to understand life and what is happening all around us. Why disease, why death, why sickness and why me? In the whole picture, though, we are significant in so many ways. We are part of a great plan He has for the world to see His love through us.

My husband and I use to enjoy our morning coffee at home until my taste buds changed due to chemotherapy. We started having our morning coffee instead at McDonolds because it seemed so much better. As a result, we met strangers that became friends, all because of cancer. To this day, we remain in contact with each other, inquiring about our well-being. We have a common knowledge and understanding of the disease.

---

[3] (Dehaan)

A demonstration of love is shown when you care and reach out to someone you do not even know, perhaps while enjoying a cup of coffee at McDonalds. We need to be receptive and sensitive to the love of others.

Friends are sometimes very distraught in regards to my cancer, and they approach me as if my life were over. The word cancer seems to be associated with a death sentence. However, it is not over with me, until the end. Hope is the word I want to leave with each survivor. Life may only begin for some when they get cancer because it is only then that they view life in the right perspective. It can make you a better person and life can be fulfilling.

This is the reason that love is the first chapter of this book. Survivors need support. I want to be there for them. I want to be used by God to encourage those that need it.

Supporting Love

Our last subtopic under "The Rose" or the love of God manifested is the connection survivors have with each other. Survivors know what the other person is either going through or is about to experience. There is mutual understanding that creates a bond and a concern one for the other. All we have to know about someone is what stage of cancer or what kind. At this point, we have read up on all sorts of diseases, their statistics, and the protocol for treatment. Survivors become very knowledgeable about procedures, treatment centers, effective cancer chemotherapy, and definitively the lingering effects patients experience after treatment.

We attend a "Cancer Care Group" in Fort Lauderdale. This is a support group of either survivors or caregivers that meet on a regular basis. Some have been going for ten years or more to either receive support or to give it to someone who needs it. The warmth of Christian compassion, care and love is very evident. The mutual concern for each other is very precious. Oh, the ties that bind us! A forty mile round trip to this care group is worth every minute spent in good Christian fellowship. It is amazing how complete strangers can become dear friends for a lifetime.

According to "The American Cancer Society" *One clinical trial found that support groups helped reduce tension, anxiety, fatigue, and confusion. Some research has shown that there is a link between group support and greater tolerance of cancer treatment and ability to follow treatment plans. One psychologist found that an educational, supportive intervention resulted in more patients taking their medicines as prescribed, which led to an increase in survival rates.*[4]

Look around and reach out to those in need. In return, you will be blessed and perhaps, you may be the only person that would ever impact another's life.

---

[4] (Society, Support Groups, What is the evidence?)

Notes and thoughts on
"The Rose."

_____

_____

_____

_____

_____

_____

_____

_____

_____

_____

_____

_____

_____

_____

_____

_____

_____

_____

_____

_____

_____

_____

_____

_____

_____

_____

_____

Chapter 2

"The Gates."

New Territory

The open gates in the painting signify entrance to new territory. As I walk through the gate of my new life, I am overwhelmed, yet struck with awe. The physical part of this disease is a fight for life. The awesome aspect of this battle is the spiritual journey. God's presence, love, peace, and purpose are felt in ways that could never have otherwise been experienced. In the post-cancer journey, my husband takes my hand, and we walk together facing the good and bad times. He is affected by this as I am, only in a different way. As we each share our story, we desire to share our story of hope.

If I had a magic pill that would cure cancer, I am sure that most everyone would try that medicine. That would take care of the physical part, but unfortunately, there is no such pill so we try treatment after treatment with the hope that this will extend life.

We also have a spiritual part to us and for that, there is a remedy. God has given us His Word, the Bible, which is absolute truth and contains all of the answers about life. Our eternity is of much greater importance than life here on earth, which is just a vapor. But eternal life is forever, either with God or separated from Him. Most of us do not want to talk about death, but the truth is, if you were born, you will die. We cannot change that any more than we can change the fact that there is a God who loves us and made a way for us to spend eternity with Him in heaven. So our hope and prayer is that anyone who has not settled things with God may do so while they have the opportunity. If you ask God to reveal Himself to you, He will! Then His Word will come alive, and He will change your life.

As I pass through the gate, I begin my physical battle with cancer and my spiritual journey, which consists of a personal relationship with God. What an exciting adventure to have. In this new avenue of life, there are many unknowns. Nobody knows what lies ahead. Cancer will change your life forever and you will relate better with those in the same situation. You have left behind life as you knew it. From now on, the way people speak to you or communicate with you will be different. God knows everything about what is happening and He does care about you.

The presence of God does not begin just because you have passed through the gates. The beautiful fact is that you are not alone. He was just as present, loving, and graceful, before you became sick, but you are probably only realizing the importance of His presence now. Those that have confidence in God, look to Him as the Shepherd of their lives. Survivors become more spiritual when facing cancer. In the 23rd Psalm verse 1 it says: **"The Lord is my Shepherd."** When you find yourself in a situation with cancer (as we have), you wonder how anyone could ever go through life without a personal relationship with God, the Shepherd.

The name given to God is a fitting one. As the Wikipedia encyclopedia says, "The Good Shepherd" *is one of the thrusts of Biblical scripture. This illustration encompasses many ideas, including God's care for his people. The tendency of humans to put themselves into dangerous situations, and their inability to guide and take care of themselves apart from the direct power and leading of God is also reinforced with the metaphor of sheep in need of a shepherd."*[5]

The following Bible verses all refer to Jesus as the Good Shepherd.
John 10:11 Jesus says, I Am the **good Shepherd**.
Hebrews 13:20. (Jesus, that **great Shepherd** of the sheep).
1 Peter 2:25. (The **Shepherd** and Bishop of your souls).
1 Peter 5:4. (The **chief Shepherd**).

I was in desperate need of help. I needed God to be my guide and to take me by the hand. With a feeling of despair, and sometimes on the verge of panic, I soon realized, I was not alone. I have learned more about God and His beautiful attributes as a result of my experience with cancer. In that sense, I can say that I would not have wanted to go through life any other way. Therefore, I am thankful for what has happened to me.

Life is a journey. Cancer can awaken our thoughts and touch our emotions to stir our soul. Living with the disease is only a segment of life's journey, yet it makes a big difference

---

[5] (http://en.wikipedia.org/wiki/Shepherd)

how we choose to live it, which determines the final outcome. I want to remind you again, there is hope while dealing with cancer. My greatest desire is to help others know "the hope" and the many blessings God has for them.

In some cases, because of my sickness, many do not know what to say to me. It is easier for some to distance themselves, rather than trying to deal with a disease they do not understand. We cannot blame them for that. Before I became a cancer survivor myself, I had those same feelings. We must learn to understand them and accept the changes that exist on this side of the gate. I would not want you to think for a moment that this side is worse than the other. We have so much to be thankful for all that lies ahead of us. I will say that your life can be more fulfilled on this side because of what it will make of you.

I am sure that you now appreciate life much more than you ever did. Isn't life a challenge and a blessing? It is so precious to get up in the morning and breathe the fresh morning air. Life means so much more today than it did before cancer. Sometimes I like to use the abbreviation B.C. before cancer. However, that would take away the actual value of what it was meant to be.

The first words of Psalm 23 have been repeated over and again in almost every aspect of misfortune or disaster. No one even questions the preciousness of the Shepherd, or the comforting truths it represents. It is sad to find this reiterated only at times of disaster like at a funeral, or at the bedside in a hospital.

According to a study, "The Bible in American Life," conducted by the Center for the Study of Religion and American Culture, 50% of Americans read some form of scripture in the past year, and 48% of those read the Bible.

Four in 5 read it at least once a month, and 9% of Americans say they read the Bible daily. The study continued to say: Consulting Scripture for personal prayer is three times more common than turning to the Bible to learn about controversial issues like abortion, homosexuality, war or poverty. Nearly half of the 48% who do read the Bible on their own said they turned most favorably to the Book of Psalms, particularly noting Psalm 23, which begins "the Lord is my shepherd."[6]

The knowledge of the Shepherd must be during our daily lives and not just at the end of it. Surely if the Good Shepherd is not known during our lifetime, it is a wasted life. Since many have heard about the 23rd Psalm, it would be fitting now to get to know Him personally, to be able to say, the Lord is _my_ Shepherd. The Lord, has revealed Himself to me as the Shepherd in my life.

A commentator said: *In these words, the believer is taught to express his satisfaction in the care of the great Pastor of the universe, the Redeemer and Preserver of men. With joy, he reflects that he has a shepherd, and that shepherd is Jehovah. A flock of sheep, gentle and harmless, feeding in verdant pastures, under the care of a skilful, watchful, and tender shepherd, forms an emblem of believers brought back to the Shepherd of their souls. The greatest abundance is but a dry pasture to a wicked man, who relishes in it only what pleases the senses; but to a godly man, who by faith tastes the goodness of God in all his enjoyments, though he has, but little of the world, it is a green pasture. The Lord gives quiet and contentment in the mind, whatever the lot is.*[7]

---

[6] (University)
[7] (Henry)

From where I have lived, (the eastern part of the United States), I am unfamiliar with shepherds leading their flock. I have read about them and seen nativity scenes every Christmas. A full understanding of a shepherd's activity is probably unknown to many of us. David, the author of this Psalm, was a shepherd and experienced many dangerous situations. During Bible times, shepherds were part of the landscape and way of life. Sheep are still popular today for their wool and meat. The important role of the shepherd is to protect sheep from predators and lead them to pastures that satisfy their needs. Shepherds are necessary because sheep by nature are unprotected and have a tendency to wander off away from the flock.

We do not have a clear understanding of eternity or about the spirit or soul, yet, we have the audacity to declare God dead and remove Him and the Bible from the schools. To only have man's limited ideas of life is to be left in complete ignorance like sheep without a shepherd. Thank God that He has revealed Himself through the Bible. He is alive and the Shepherd of all who believe, as depicted in the 23rd Psalm. I am thrilled every day when I can learn more about Him by reading His message to us, the Bible.

Spiritual Experience

Sometimes it takes a tragedy in our lives to help us realize the real reason for living and why He wants to be our Shepherd. He desires to lead, protect, give hope, and show us that nothing is too big or small for Him. Now that I have passed through the other side of the gates, my perspective on life has changed. As a result of the trials and sufferings, life is seen in a different light. Personal values change as wisdom sets in our hearts. If it takes trials to bring us to that point, it is good.

Survivors often are more receptive towards spiritual things when confronted with a life-and–death situation. I have realized that "time" is of the essence. "Time" is precious, it is limited, time is short, fleeting and before we know it, it is all gone. James 4:14 says: *"Whereas ye know not what shall be on the morrow. For what is your life? It is even a vapour that appeareth for a little time, and then vanisheth away."* Psalm 90:12 says: *"So teach us to number our days that we may apply our hearts unto wisdom."*

I realize the brevity of life and the frailty of my body. The procedures to get cancer under control, is very difficult to endure. The continual endurance attacks the moral being of a patient, which temps one to give up trying to stay alive.

Chemotherapy strips us of all dignity, and humiliates us because of our appearance. We become fragile, weak, and sick. We look and feel like aliens, but God loves us regardless and will see us through. I have lost my hair three times in the past five years due to chemotherapy. *Traditional chemotherapies work by killing cells that divide rapidly. However, as they wipe out fast-growing cancer cells, they also can damage fast-growing healthy cells.*

Damage to healthy blood cells, for example, can lead to side effects such as fatigue or infection. Chemotherapy can also damage the cells that line mucous membranes throughout the body, including those inside the mouth, throat and stomach. This can lead to mouth sores, diarrhea or other issues with the digestive system. And damage to cells at the hair roots or follicles, can lead to hair loss.[8]

---

[8] (Care)

Inner Beauty

God is interested in developing our inner beauty. The journey before us accomplishes this goal. I Samuel 16:7 says: *"for the LORD seeth not as man seeth. For man looketh on the outward appearance, but the LORD looketh on the heart."* Focusing on the peace and joy of the Lord in our heart can help us deal with our physical appearance. Often people have a false sense of inward security, relying on the outward appearance which is fleeting. Attractive movie stars and models can become depressed and suicidal because they lack the beautiful inner peace only found in God. This is not to say that efforts should not be made to look your best. There are programs to help one cope with the effects of chemotherapy. Like, "look good, feel good" programs. Our self-esteem is attacked, and it is hard to adjust, but so reassuring to know that the Creator is looking at our inner beauty. Once we have cancer, we are on the other side of an imaginary line, yet it is real in the application. This side is a time of change and adaptation to many aspects of life. Those issues can affect how you feel, look, and live.

The Vanderbilt-Ingram Cancer Center says it this way on their site. *Cancer, treatment, and their side effects can dramatically alter the appearance. How you look might change temporarily (losing your hair or gaining weight due to chemotherapy, having redness or swelling due to radiation) or permanently (changes in body shape or appearance due to surgery). Our appearance is important to us, and how a treatment affects our appearance is a factor for many people when choosing a treatment.*

Sometimes people dealing with cancer and its treatment find that they start to think of themselves differently as a result of changes in their body appearance or their self-image. People might start to see themselves as less attractive after cancer or surgery, even if other people would not agree. They might start to question whether their bodies work properly. Also, sometimes just the knowledge that a person has cancer can make them think about themselves and their bodies differently like they cannot rely on their bodies or trust them anymore. [9]

What you think about yourself is imperative. Sometimes professional help is needed. Many cancer centers offer counseling services for problems, such as anger and irritability, anxiety, depression, memory and concentration problems. Other possible issues may include low self-image and self-esteem, sexuality, sleep disruption, stress within the family or couple. These subjects affect the whole body and mind. Support groups are there to help. Getting involved in a support group collectively benefits the survivors and the caregivers. Visit a support group, it would be to your advantage. It just might be what is needed. We found that the fellowship was excellent and encouraging. Each person is different, and each need varies. What works for one person might not necessarily work for another.

Health issues, are not the only change factors that occurs for a survivor. There is the financial stress. With cancer treatments, you, your doctors and your loved ones, want to do everything possible to beat the disease. Sparing no expense, though, can be difficult, and the stress that comes with these financial challenges can take its toll. It is important to personally call your insurance company directly to get

---

[9] (Center.)

answers about your coverage. Do not rely on your doctor's office regarding your insurance program. A study from Duke Cancer Institute found that patients who bring up money issues believe that doing so helped reduce their costs. Doctors may be able to prescribe cheaper medications or refer patients to hospital assistance programs. There are internet sites to help find financial resources. Dealing with the finances is enough to stifle recuperation from the sickness itself. The stress of all the cost is overwhelming and the Shepherd is aware of the situation. God has unlimited ways and resources to direct and provide the needs of His sheep. You may be one that experiences a life changing journey, by seeing the Shepherd's promise to do all He says He does in our Psalm. The more we get to know Him, the more we realize, He is the Good Shepherd.

Cancer survivors, are those that survive cancer, and the financial burden that goes with it: Steve White, Director of Mind-Body Medicine at a hospital outside Phoenix, *says patients may experience anxiety or depression because of financial worry.*
White advises patients to manage their stress through a variety of ways:

- *Getting enough sleep*
- *Exercising*
- *Participating in activities and hobbies you enjoy*
- *Meditation*
- *Guided imagery, in which you imagine yourself in a calm place*[10]

One reason for the high costs of cancer treatment is the costs of new drugs. Of the 12 drugs approved by the Food

---

[10] (America)

and Drug Administration for cancer conditions in 2012, 11 were priced above $100,000 for a year of treatment, according to a report by TakePart.com.

At the end of this chapter you will find a resource page for financial help. There are people that care and give to help others. God can use them to meet your needs.

Our journey through cancer has many new aspects added to our lives. Our self-esteem, finances, and priorities have been put to the test. What was important prior to cancer, is now different. Certain activities of a typical day even change. I want to do things that matter in my life. The more I learn about the Good Shepherd the more I want my life to count for eternity.

Forget the exercise routine, I just wanted to be able to get up, try to feel better to face the day that was before me. My health did not permit a full day's activity or to work all day. In the morning, I had to choose the most important duties and prioritize because the afternoon was a time to recuperate, rest and try to do a little more before the end of the day. In between treatments I had to choose which days I would work at a doctor's office, and that would be only a couple of days a week. I had to decide when to visit my children and grandchildren. Afternoons were almost out of the question. Since my immune system was weak, I could not be exposed to the children while they were ill. My life revolved around priorities. Our life should be to evaluate what is important in life and to do it. So much time is wasted in doing insignificant things over and over again. The experience helped me to set my priorities right. Today I can understand the importance of letting go of all that concerns me, and letting God lead as my Shepherd. Can you say in your heart today, "The Lord is my Shepherd"?

Knowing The Shepherd

To succeed on this journey, we must learn to let God be the Shepherd that leads and speaks to us. Peter Graystone, in his book "Ready Salted" has an illustration that says:

A man fell over a cliff and, as he tumbled down the sheer drop, managed to grab on to a scrubby bush growing from the side of the rock. Terrified, he hung in space, his life flashing before him. In desperation, he shouted toward heaven, 'Is there anyone up there?'

To his astonished delight, a voice floated down: 'I am the Lord God, and I am here.'

'What should I do?' called the man.

The voice replied, 'Let go of the branch and, with my protection, you will float harmlessly down to the beach below.'

The man glanced under his feet to the jagged rocks at the foot of the cliff, hundreds of meters below. He gulped, and looked back toward heaven. 'Well... is there anyone else up there?'

Not only do we have problems with personal values, self-esteem, priorities, but with cancer diagnosis there are also fears. The greatest of these fears is death. The thought is always there. Any trip to the doctor's office causes apprehension, wondering if it is good news or not. The element of fear is triggered, not only when you see a doctor, but when new symptoms appear. I always question if it is normal. The bad news is interpreted in our minds as a step closer to death. I think this is a natural reaction. I believe it is in the heart of mankind to want to live. Life is a beautiful thing. No one likes to suffer or have difficulties. The desire to live helps us persevere in fighting cancer. Thankfully, having the Good Shepherd to rely on takes away much stress. We are reminded in scriptures that we are not to worry. Matthew 6:25-26 says:

[25] "Therefore I say unto you, Take no thought for your life, what ye shall eat, or what ye shall drink; nor yet for your body, what ye shall put on. Is not the life more than meat, and the body than raiment?

[26] Behold the fowls of the air: for they sow not, neither do they reap nor gather into barns; yet your heavenly Father feedeth them. Are ye not much better than they?"

The Good Shepherd is the only one that can totally take care of us to the end. When any temptation comes our way, then, it is our duty to look to him for deliverance and victory. I often wonder how anyone can go through life not knowing the God of the Bible. How can anyone make an accurate conclusion about his or her life and the hereafter? You would have to be God and know everything, from the beginning to the end for all creatures. Some have taken on this evaluation and come to the conclusion that there is no God. The Bible says in Psalms 14:1 "The fool hath said in his heart, There is no God."

Survivors of any traumatic experience are prone to be sensitive to the spiritual world and the afterlife. Rarely do they deny God's existence. We believe in a living God that has a close relationship with us just like a good shepherd has with his sheep. The Good Shepherd is there when we fear anything, like death, bad news, operations, exams, and, chemotherapy.

The National Coalition For Cancer Survivorship says; *there are three major cancer-related fears described in the research literature. These are fear of death, fear of recurrence and fear of stigma, which is fear of being thought about or treated differently.*

The following article is a summation about the fear of stigma.

The disease of cancer still carries a stigma. Despite treatment advances and extended survival rates for many cancers, cancer remains a stigmatized disease, and persons with cancer must contend with societal attitudes, prejudices and discrimination solely on the basis of their cancer history. The stress of a diagnosis of cancer and its subsequent treatment requires many personal and interpersonal changes. For example, during the treatment phase, there may have been a redistribution of tasks within your family unit and these functions may need to be renegotiated. There also may be significant changes in your relationships with friends and acquaintances. Now that you have been diagnosed with cancer, people you know may respond to you differently. They may negatively stereotype you as a "cancer victim" or believe that your cancer is an automatic death sentence.

Returning to work also may create various stresses. There may be a difference in the way coworkers treat a person who has been absent, even briefly, due to cancer. They may avoid you or isolate you. Also, due to a lack of understanding, ignorance or fear about cancer, many individuals with a cancer history experience some form of employment discrimination such as dismissal, demotion, or failure to get a promotion or new job.

The challenges and tasks of living with cancer are many. Perhaps most important of all these tasks is learning to live with uncertainty while maintaining a functional and optimal level of hope.

As a conclusion to this Chapter on the "gate" and the Good Shepherd, who guides us along the journey, let me encourage you to look to God for strength and direction in all things. Get to know the Lord by reading the Holy Bible. Get to know the Good Shepherd as Lord and Savior. He loved you and gave all the proof of His love at the cross of Calvary. He invites you when he says in Matthew 11:28: "Come unto me, all *ye* that labour and are heavy laden, and I will give you rest."
In John 3:16 it is written, "For God so loved the world, that he gave his only begotten Son, that whosoever believeth in him should not perish but have everlasting life."

Today, if you bow your head in prayer and ask God to forgive you of your past, your failures, your sins, He will hear you. If you invite Him into your life and your heart, realizing that He paid the total debt of sin on the cross for you, the Good Shepherd will accept you unto Himself. He will lead you in everything that He promises in Psalm 23. If you make this personal commitment, we are on the same path with the same Shepherd and Savior.

Resource Page For Financial Aid

Following is a list of foundations that you can find on our website at HopeThroughCancer.com. Each one has a link. Check them out. You might qualify for financial aid.

1. People being treated for metastatic breast cancer may be eligible to receive up to $10,000 for co-payment assistance per year through the Cancer Care Co-Payment Assistance Foundation.

2. The PAF Co-Pay Relief Program, one of the self-contained divisions of PAF, provides direct financial assistance to insured patients who meet certain qualifications to help them pay for the prescriptions and/or treatments they need.

3. The Ulman Cancer Fund offers two types of navigation for young adult cancer patients (18-40 years old) and survivors-remote and on-site. All services are FREE of charge and open to family members and loved ones.

4. The AbbVie Patient Assistance Foundation provides AbbVie medicines at no cost to qualified patients who are experiencing financial difficulties and who generally do not have coverage available for these products through private insurance or government funded programs.

Notes and thoughts on:
"The Gate."

_____
_____
_____
_____
_____
_____
_____
_____
_____
_____
_____
_____
_____
_____
_____
_____
_____
_____
_____
_____
_____
_____
_____
_____
_____
_____
_____
_____

Chapter 3
"The Path."

*Psalm 23: 3 says: "**He leaded me in the paths of righteousness for His name's sake.**"*

    This part of the painting shows a path, symbolizing what is ahead. The first part of this chapter explains the "Path" and the second part describes how He leads with truths of righteousness.

The Path

    What path are we talking about in this verse? What is the context that helps us understand what we are dealing with? We take many different roads during our lifetime. Every path chosen is the result of a decision made, either with negligence or according to our best knowledge. Life is a series of choices.

When the Lord is our Shepherd, He will lead on the right paths. This Psalm was written by David and suggests that there was a time in David's life that he did not know the Shepherd as such. It also suggests that he did not always know God in a personal way. David probably was taught the Old Testament or what they did possess at the time of his writing this Psalm. He was taught by his father Jesse, who was an example to him. I believe that David came to know the Lord as Shepherd and Savior when he was young. Perhaps when he started caring for sheep and spending time alone in the deserts and wilderness, he reflected on his father's teachings. He had the stars, sun, and the moon to remind him of God. With little distractions, other than having the responsibilities of being a shepherd, David had ample time on his hand to meditate God's Word. He became very personal with God. In his Psalm, he later referred to Him as the Good Shepherd. David grew up strong and brave, not afraid of the wild beasts that prowled and tried to carry away his sheep. More than once he fought lions and bears and killed them when they seized the lambs of his flock. Also David, alone all day, practiced throwing stones in a sling until he could strike exactly the place for which he aimed. When he swung his sling, he had confidence that the stone would go to the very spot he intended. God watched over David and they had fellowship together.

At a young age, David learned the truths concerning the Good Shepherd, and believed in Him with all his heart. He found purpose to live by those truths. Not everyone can say the Lord is "**my** Shepherd." I was ten years old when he became my Lord, Savior, and Shepherd. It is not enough to know about the Shepherd, and not enough to know that He is good. I invite you to accept the Lord and Shepherd, in your heart for a personal relationship with Him.

Having the Lord as Shepherd means so much and holds the greatest truths that man could ever dwell on. There are many truths about the Shepherd in this Psalm. The message of the whole Bible can be summed up in this Psalm and all that it implies. I thank God that he has revealed Himself to me and drew me to a saving knowledge of the Savior of my soul. I was taught the Bible and every story in it. I went to Sunday school every week. Finally, I understood the grace that God had for me. The very fact that you are reading this book may be God's way of speaking to you from my experience. There is a path before us. We either adjust to it or we become very bitter about our situation concerning cancer.

Life's journey is at the same time long and viewed in retrospect, very short. The older I become, the faster time flies. At one time, I thought that the school year took an eternity before coming to the summer months for vacation. Now the years are moving so quickly. Looking back, I see life as a flash of light. We often say, "this too shall pass,"and my cancer battle will also pass. However, time has become precious. I am on a path with the one that made me and is in full control of my life. He is the Good Shepherd, and I am counting on Him, like a weak sheep needing someone to lead. I am living with a disease that can shorten the years, but they will not be shorter or longer than God allows.

The journey with cancer is filled with the routine of tedious tasks. I now have to remember so many things I did not have to deal with before. I must remember the frailty of my body and not subject it to more than it can handle. Otherwise, I pay the consequences very quickly. Have you noticed how many doctors appointments you have? One for the chemotherapy, one for follow-up, another for a shot. Always going back to the doctor for the results, which is troubling and tiresome. Chemotherapy is about every three weeks. After chemo, come the blood tests, scans, back to the doctor for results, always hoping for the best yet fearing the worst. It is an emotional roller coaster. No wonder I am exhausted most of the time.

I found it helpful to keep a diary to document how I was feeling, listing medications and side effects. It is valuable to keep a journal to record the reactions of my body, like blood pressure every morning. I documented when I felt nauseous, constipated, headache, backache or neuropathy. I also wrote down questions for the next doctor's visit. One new major task was taking all the pills at the right time for the prescribed purpose. I usually write down the ones taken and with chemo-brain, I sometimes wonder if I wrote it down. I have used pill boxes, morning and afternoon slots to help me remember. To succeed, I ask my husband to remind me to take a particular medicine at a certain time. I also take supplements to help build the immune system, and it goes on and on. At this point, I am exhausted with the mental pressure of all the tasks.

Imagine adding in another factor, like visitors coming to the house on short notice. It takes everything, to get going and just live. It is not easy to have a positive attitude. Now I must make the bed, clean the dishes, pick up clothes, straighten up the house or just close the bedroom door. In some areas, I would just like to close the door and put up a sign that says "please do not enter." I appreciate all my husband does to help. Together we are an excellent team. We support each other as we deal with the many changes that are before us.

As a survivor, I have lost my hair for the third time. Most of my life I wasn't conscious of hair. People who are not survivors have no idea of the new world we live in because of cancer. One day I was going to the grocery store to pick up a couple of items. When I got into the car, I felt a draft around my head and neck. I realized my head was bare naked and quickly ran back to get my baseball cap. When I visited my granddaughter, and I only had my hat on, and left my wig at home, my granddaughter looked at me and said: "grandmom, could you bring your hair next time?" I laughed. I am continually reminded of the many new changes on this journey.

With cancer, the daunting fear of recurrence is always present. Even though we face all kinds of trials every day, some trivial and some burdensome, It is like having our own "fear factor" show. There is a new fear factor every day. There is fear of recurrences, fear of another operation, and fear of something going wrong. I need strength from above to be able to put these thoughts in the background of my mind, and re-member that the Shepherd knows all about it and is taking care of it all.

This is where I must look to my Lord for help and strength. He does not want me to worry about anything. His desire is to satisfy me with His presence, His words, and His promises. I deal with this through prayer and meditation of His Word. My husband and I, every morning, read a portion of the Bible, read a couple meditational books, and we pray on our knees for help and the provisions we need. We come to the Good Shepherd and place our desires at His feet, at the throne of grace. Prayer is a great privilege that the Shepherd has given us.

The journey before us is a special one, not because of all the negative facts about cancer, but it is special because there are many positive aspects of having cancer. It is not healthy to have a negative attitude. There are no benefits at all in being cynical about our situation. There is a poem entitled "What Cancer Cannot Do." It supposedly first appeared in the 1960's in an Ann Landers column. It is inspiring.

What Cancer Cannot Do
Cancer is so limited...
It cannot cripple love.
It cannot shatter hope.
It cannot corrode faith.
It cannot destroy peace.
It cannot kill friendship(s).
It cannot suppress memories.
It cannot silence courage.
It cannot invade the soul.
It cannot steal eternal life.
It cannot conquer the spirit.

-Author Unknown

I find that having cancer opens many new avenues of opportunities. Look at cancer as a time to explore new possibilities in life. This is how I dealt with it. I hope that you will reflect on my positive experiences and see your world of opportunities. Cancer cannot take away opportunities, but it can permit you to see possibilities that you would not have otherwise considered. What did it do to me? It changed my thinking and my life.

The first thought that came to me was, what could I do for others? I saw what others were doing for me and the concerns they had. However, my heart was burdened for those that were in the same situation. I was encouraged by my husband, my children, and my Lord. I thought that in reality, not many have the support they need. So I wanted to help by talking to them, sharing my story, and maybe giving something to encourage them. My nursing background helped me communicate with patients. Not only did I know the many medical terms and procedures, I was also a survivor.

Encouragement in life is an element as important as eating or drinking. Without support, a person can fall into a deep depression that affects health. I want to encourage and inspire you to find your journey with cancer, as a time to reorganize your life to be better than ever. It can happen. Believe the Shepherd and follow Him, for surely He will lead you on a fulfilled path of righteousness. Maybe this poem will bless you as it did me. This is from an anonymous writer taken from online.[11]

"When things go wrong as they sometimes will,
When the road you're trudging seems all up hill,
When the funds are low and the debts are high
And you want to smile, but you have to sigh,
When care is pressing you down a bit,
Rest if you must, but don't you quit.
Life is queer with its twists and turns,
As every one of us sometimes learns,
And many a failure turns about
When he might have won had he stuck it out;
Don't give up though the pace seems slow--
You may succeed with another blow,
Success is failure turned inside out--
The silver tint of the clouds of doubt,
And you never can tell how close you are,

---

[11] Unknown

48

It may be near when it seems so far;
So stick to the fight when you're hardest hit--
It's when things seem worst that you must not quit."

~ Author Unknown

How He leads with truths of righteousness.

I did not want to stop living. I just wanted a fulfilled God fearing life, reaching out to touch the lives of others for God's glory. I needed a close relationship with the Shepherd to know what plans He had for me. We have experienced closed doors and open doors on our journey. Alexander Graham Bell said; "When one door closes another door opens; but we so often look so long and so regretfully upon the closed door that we do not see the ones that open for us."

A door to ordinary living is now closed. We can focus on what happened or we can look ahead to new opportunities. There are plenty before us. We cannot do them all, so why not choose something and go for it. There are two avenues of opportunities. It can be for ourselves or for others. Life has to be more than just what we want to do for ourselves. What is it that we need so badly that we cannot look further to see others and consider them? What will we be remembered by after we have left this world? Will it be how wonderfully we took care of ourselves or how sensitive we were towards others and their needs? I believe that I must love and give back to the unloved and the needy. H. Jackson Brown Jr. said: "Remember that the happiest people are not those getting more, but those giving more." [12]

Philosopher Howard Thurman said:

---

[12] (Brown)

"Don't ask what the world needs. Ask what makes you come alive, and go do it. Because what the world needs is people who have come alive." Our paths of opportunities permit us to evaluate fully our lives our actions and to live the rest of it entirely. We should orient our activities not so much as how much we take but how much we give. ***"Define your life in terms of giving rather than taking****: You don't have to be a rich philanthropist with your name on a wall to be remembered. Do what you can; give with all your heart. Lives defined by generosity make indelible marks on history.* [13]

Claude and I came up with the idea of doing an oil painting that could represent my journey. He wanted to oil paint on canvas when he retired. His sister bought him a kit for oil painting. He was inspired to start right away, about six years earlier than planned. He took courses online, spent time with an artist, and was on his way. He was consumed and surprised with the talent he had. We started wondering what I could do as a past time. Nothing worthwhile came to mind until I remembered a gift from long ago from my sister in law.

She gave me a rag quilt, and I pondered "maybe" sewing for a pass time. We started on a great mission. He believed in me and was sure I could learn. No one is born a sewer; they have to learn how to sew. So we had to find a sewing machine. We had fun shopping and dreaming of what we could accomplish. The time spent searching distracted my thoughts away from cancer. I was on a mission, and I was going to learn to sew. We realized it was a special time together. I had cancer, and we were doing something exciting. This joy bubbled inside me as I thought of making others happy.

---

[13] (Merill)

I needed sewing lessons to learn first of all, how to use a sewing machine, especially with all the new computerized programs and gadgets. Finally, I was making rag quilts. I surprised myself that I succeeded. The family was proud of my accomplishments. I was proud of myself; it made me feel good and happy. My greatest joy was when I gave one to my husband, to my kids, grandchildren, and my first one to a cancer survivor.

Every time that we give a rag quilt, I am reminded of the story my husband told about when he was about fifteen years of age. He and his friend decided to go to Ontario, Canada, and work in the tobacco fields. Let me say at this point that his convictions are such, that today he would not support the industry. They were living in Quebec, Canada at the time. They bought themselves a one-way train ticket with just enough money to come home if everything went wrong. This was the first time both of them went to work 500 miles away from home. Things did not start off well because they arrived a couple of weeks before the crops were ready for harvest.

There were hundreds of workers that found themselves in the same situation, destitute of work and money. The towns were in unrest because of street gangs and break-ins. By the time they got to their city, many hotels and motels had no vacancy. One private home, which rented out rooms told them they had no vacancy, but reluctantly offered them an old "closed in" trailer, about 10 feet long. It was better than being outside in the damp summer cold nights and mornings. They slept but calculated they could not afford twelve dollars a night.

Early the next morning they took off taking the blanket with them. They stole the blanket. He has often said; he did a terrible thing to those people. If it were possible, he would reimburse them and the trouble caused by taking their blanket. They did their best to accommodate them, and they turned around and ripped them off. Nothing could justify stealing a blanket. They wanted to be sure to have enough money to make it back home if things got worse.

For the next week or so they slept in a nearby patch of woods off from the golf course. They gathered dry grass for their pillow and covered up the best they could at night. Very thankful for the blanket, yet feeling very guilty for what they did. They were able to survive by keeping a loaf of bread and peanut butter hidden in the woods, and that was their food morning and night. When the dew came down about three or four o'clock in the morning, they would go to the nearest coffee shop to get warmed up with coffee.

Claude is always thankful to this day when we can give a rag quilt to anyone in need. The wrong actions for a blanket made him remorseful and then, grateful to be able to give back and help others. What a privilege. There are things in life that remind us of our past. It is wonderful that the Good Shepherd forgives and continues to lead His sheep.

I found a post on a website that said it this way. *Hobbies provide a number of important benefits. They provide us a break from responsibilities and work and give us an outlet to use our free time to do something we love or care about. Many hobbies, such as group sports, book clubs, or other social pastimes give us an opportunity to expand our social circles and have a social life outside of our families and co-workers (which any busy parent can tell you is important to do once in a while).*

Psychologically, performing an activity that gives you pleasure, such as playing music or golfing, gives you a boost and brings joy to your life. If you want more happiness and less stress, hobbies are a valuable tool in achieving that. In addition, hobbies help to rejuvenate our senses and keep stress overload at bay. If your job is overwhelmingly busy on a regular basis, a few hours a week recharging through a favorite pastime is extremely valuable.[14]

The questions lie before you. What can you do to occupy your thoughts and be happy with yourself? You can start something new like I did, and pursue that desire. Some people have become very creative about how to help others. There are plenty of opportunities. If your mind can shift from only looking at yourself and turning to others, then, you can find a certain fulfillment. Cancer survivors often want to reach out to others with cancer and help them through the cancer experience by supporting, listening, and sharing their personal stories. It can involve contacting them or visiting them. However, there are so many ways to help and support. Some volunteer for a cancer walk fundraising event, or buy products ranging from clothing to postage stamps, from organizations that set aside a portion of the money to support the cause.

The following hobbies could be worth looking into. **Domonique Chardon** wrote this on one of her guest blogs: Here are three hobbies that can help others, as well as your self-esteem.

Volunteering: Whether you're helping out with a local organization, raising awareness for a particular cause or fundraising on an issue you believe in — volunteering is an

---

[14] (The Importance Of Hobbies And Stress Relief)

extremely fulfilling hobby. Getting familiar with issues in your community and more importantly the people and organizations behind them, is an excellent way to give back and also benefit from the experience. It's also an excellent way to make new friends and meet new people that you might not otherwise run into. A kind heart is always remembered.

Baking: You'd be surprised how far one cupcake will go! Baking is a fantastic hobby that does require some skill and a penchant for hitting the sweet spot; but what I love the most about baking is: I'm not the only one who can enjoy the results! One may not notice at first, but there are plenty of opportunities to apply baking skills. Aside from baking for special occasions like birthdays etc., I'm a firm believer that any day is a good day for a cupcake! Or a cookie, or cake, or cake pops, or brownies, you get my drift. The Baker is adored.

Physical Challenge: Let's face it – not all of us were born athletes or are where we want to be in terms of physical fitness. That's why choosing a physical challenge as a hobby is difficult; however, it can be most rewarding. Besides improving your health, another upside is the various options one can choose from. There's literally something for everyone. If you don't enjoy working out in a gym you can hike, bike or run outdoors. Why not join team training, a road race, an organized walk or a marathon where all the proceeds go to a great cause. Knowing that you are doing it for others will help push you along. It's a win-win situation. When you challenge your body, you also challenge your mind. It takes determination to commit to practicing a physical hobby regularly. As your stamina builds, you will become even more determined and you will see results![15]

To say the least, and as you have already experienced, we are on a journey with a new way of life. This life is new in many ways, for example; it is a world of doctors, medicine, pills, chemotherapy, physical and mental stress. We now have new hats, wigs, new clothes to adjust to our ever changing body, sickness, weakness, emotional stress, different kinds of food, diets, and friends. We even talk differently. We talk to those that understand what is going on and try to get as much encouragement as possible. It is a path for survivorship. It is nothing chosen by desire but given to us for a reason. There is a divine reason why we are where we are. I try to make the best of life and what is left. It is most likely better to have the quality of life than quantity. Many people have lived years, are old, have had good health, yet never learned to live a purposeful life that would count for something in the afterlife. The things that last for eternity are not the usual activities of life, but the things done for Christ and others for His sake.

M.R. De Haan said it right in one of his devotionals; Living or Just Alive?

What matters is not how long you live, but how well you live. Some people live for 85 years and do very little. Others live only a relatively few years, but they fill that time with service to God and others, and their influence lives on. Many people are concerned only with prolonging their stay here on this earth, and so they strive to add years to their lives. Every year we spend billions of dollars for medicines, vitamins, and special diets to stay alive. And yet we forget that it is not the quantity of life but the quality of life and what we accomplish

---

[15] (Chardon)

for the Lord that makes life meaningful. Only when we devote our lives to our Creator (Ecclesiastes 12:1,13-14) do our days on earth count for eternity.

Today, let's seek to fill the hours with service, worship and work for the Master. If this is our last day (and who knows, it may be), rather than wasting it in dreaming of a long life, let it be occupied with producing abundant fruit and being a blessing. Instead of just drifting aimlessly through our allotted hours and days, let us truly live. It is better to add life to your years than to add years to your life. [16]

Realizing the preciousness of time helps me to grasp the reality of life itself. Having cancer brings you to the edge of a cliff, instead of seeing the canyon from far. On the side of the cliff, you grasp the brevity of the journey and of life. Many people try to console you by saying that even they could be hit by a truck and die that day. What they do not understand is, a Mack truck has not hit them but me. I am suffering the consequences of cancer. So far, I have battled for six years. However, what some go through when the Doctors tell them there is nothing more they can do. For now this is not true of my experience. The day may come when I am at the final stage of cancer. Only then will I know what it feels like. It is difficult to think of such a day but, the strength the Shepherd gives will be sufficient .We do not know the struggles of those around us, or the various devastating situations our fellow humans may be going through. We need to be sensitive to others, reaching out, helping and endeavoring to lighten burdened hearts.

The National Health Institute says: *Those who have gone through cancer treatment describe the first few months as a*

---

[16] (M.R.Dehaan)

time of change. It is not so much "getting back to normal" as it is finding out what's normal for you now. People often say that life has new meaning or that they look at things differently now. You can also expect things to keep changing as you begin your recovery. Your new "normal" may include making changes in the way you eat, the things you do, and your sources of support.[17]

The following chapters will help us understand what to expect on our journey and what can be accomplished. Having the Good Shepherd, life will be complete, fulfilled and satisfying.

Thus far we have seen the rose symbolizing God's love; the Gate as the place of entering new territory; and the path on which we have never walked. The journey is before us, and we cannot change it. Now we will learn about the different obstacles we encounter represented by "the Branch."

---

[17] (Services)

Notes and thoughts on:

"The Path."

_____
_____
_____
_____
_____
_____
_____
_____
_____
_____
_____
_____
_____
_____
_____
_____
_____
_____
_____
_____
_____
_____
_____

CHAPTER 4
"The Branch."

Notice in the painting, the presence of a branch on the path. The chapter introduces the fourth verse of Psalm 23; **"thy rod and thy staff they comfort me."** Above all, is the promise of comfort which is based on the capacity of the Shepherd to protect and lead. Though there are dangerous areas in life, there is protection promised to His child just like a shepherd takes care of his sheep.

The rod was to safeguard both himself and his flock in danger. And it was, furthermore, the instrument he used to discipline and correct any wayward sheep that insisted on wandering away. The skilled shepherd uses his rod to drive off predators like coyotes, wolves, cougars or stray dogs. Often it is used to beat the brush discouraging snakes and other creatures from disturbing the flock. In extreme cases, such as David recounted to Saul, the psalmist no doubt used his rod to attack the lion and the bear that came to raid his flocks. The staff is essentially a symbol of the concern, the compassion that a shepherd has for his charges. No other single word can better describe its function on behalf of the flock than that it is for their "comfort." The staff is used by the shepherd to reach out and catch individual sheep, young or old and draw them close to himself for intimate examination. The staff is very useful this way for the shy and timid sheep normally tend to keep at a distance from the shepherd.[18]

The shepherd's staff was made from a tree branch having a hook the right size to put around a sheep's head. The Shepherd could pull it away from danger or lift it up from a cliff after having strayed away from the path.

In the artist's perception the branch represents problems we encounter with diagnosis and the solution promised by the keeper of our souls. *Notice, the branch is not a palm branch which is a symbol of victory, triumph, peace, and eternal life originating in the ancient Near East and the Mediterranean world.* [19] You may remember the triumphant entry of Jesus into Jerusalem, remembered as Palm Sunday. The branch is not an olive branch, a symbol of peace and hope from the biblical story of Noah's Ark.

The branch in the painting represents obstacles on our journey. After a storm or a hurricane, branches on roads stop the normal flow of traffic. We know that, during our life, there are many variations and adjustments needed to clear the way and make progress. We are in a storm with many obstacles. We must not forget the Shepherd, who is leading us and knows and cares about every obstacle and hurt that could come our way.

---

[18] (Keller)

[19] (encyclopedia)

There are three obstructions or branches ahead of us: **the physical, the mental, and the spiritual** difficulties that precede discouragement if it were not for the Shepherd leading the way. We will reflect on these obstacles, in the same order.

The Physical Obstacles

The **physical** hindrance is obvious because it affects us directly. When sick, nothing else matters. My whole being revolves around how I feel. What else can come to mind when on the verge of vomiting? Can anyone quickly shift their minds back and forth from pleasant thoughts to horror? There is quite a process once chemotherapy is administered. *The cancer has received a dose of poison to stop its growth, but the vomiting center of the brain was provided with information to initiate vomiting.*[20]

There are about 80 common medications given to treat nausea, according to WebMD. By the time the right medication is prescribed, one has quite a battle to overcome, which takes away any quality of life. I did not have so much of that problem. My problem was getting the insurance company to agree to pay for the one hundred dollar "pill" that relieved nausea. Of course, it took about three of them each time.

Beside the frustration, sickness, nausea, weakness, and soreness left me walking and looking like a hundred-year-old person. I would hunch forward taking baby steps sliding each step of the way to reach the kitchen to take my medication. The cycle kept on getting worse, by taking in so much water; I had many trips to the bathroom. My aching bones and muscles did not have time to recuperate. I reflect and realize that the

---

[20] (Wikipedia, Chemoreceptor trigger zone)

Good Shepherd was looking at me. He protected me from falling and today I feel much better.

One of the physical obstruction is hair loss which can be emotionally devastating. Women consider hair their "crowning glory." It is so important, we have it cut, styled, sometimes dyed, every month. Our hair dictates that anything of complicated nature is said to be a bad hair day. What about a bad hair day, every day, because one has no hair left? Does anyone know how I feel? I am touched by the fact that the Good Shepherd knows the number of hairs on my head and the lack of. Luke 12;7 says, "But even the very hairs of your head are all numbered. Fear not, ye are of more value than many sparrows."

A bald head complicates things. Body temperature is greatly affected by the head where much heat escapes. It either sweats or has to be kept warm in winter. At night, my head would sweat, the pillow would get wet which required constantly changing the pillowcase. In public I wanted to present myself in the best way possible. The choices were limited; a wig, scarf or hat. The science of folding the scarf and making it look right was not easy, and I did not take that course of action often. I either wore a wig or a cap. Whatever I wore made no difference on a windy day. There was no string under my neck to tie and keep my hat or wig on. My hair did grow back, but I lost it three times with cancer therapy. As I am writing, it is starting to grow out again.

Losing weight is what most people try to do till they have cancer and chemotherapy. I lost so much weight that I could see my shoulder blades and ribs. All my clothes were too big, so I needed to shop which I enjoy. Thank God that He saw me as one of His sheep, no matter what my physical appearance. I am just as precious as the best fit. He looks at the heart, through the eyes of His Son, and we are perfect in His sight.

Some survivors have an opposite effect upon their bodies, and they can gain weight which is sometimes inflammation and water retention. So whatever the situation can be, the same problem exists with fitting into clothes.

Another physical hindrance is suffering. The aches and pain along with weakness left me very exhausted. The bones would become so sore, that I needed to have my back rubbed at night with arnica gel to find enough comfort to fall asleep. This natural gel was very soothing, and penetrating, with a mild smell. We try to include this in our gift bag when we visit those new to chemotherapy.

While going through therapy, one of the side effects is that the blood counts can drop in such a way, the immune system is compromised.

Everydayhealth.com says; *If you are undergoing chemotherapy, your blood work will probably show that your white cell count hits a low point or nadir, between treatments. The cell count improves as the marrow in your bones rebuilds your immune system by producing new white cells, also known as leukocytes. Your immune system includes several types of white blood cells, including granulocytes and lymphocytes, whose job is to seek and destroy dangerous germs or cells that are damaged or abnormal because of an infection or mutation.*

Neutrophils, a type of granulocyte, are the most common white cells in the blood; they help ward off the infections that are common to cancer patients. White cells also include B lymphocytes, or B cells, which produce antibodies and fight infection, and T lymphocytes, or T cells, which help regulate immune response and attack bacteria and other harmful invaders in the blood. Your doctor will probably be monitoring the number of all these cells in your blood during therapy. If your levels have not rebounded before you start your next round of treatment, he or she may give you a short break or prescribe drugs such as filgrastim (Neupogen) or the longer-lasting pegfilgrastim (Neulasta) to help your body make more white blood cells.

When your white cells are low, a small infection can quickly escalate into a serious health threat. [21]

Having a compromised immune system limited me. I tried to stay away from public areas as much as possible. Not shaking hands was a priority. I tend to be friendly and shake hands, but now I tried to refrain. I suppose I insulted some, but explaining that it was because of cancer helped others to understand. We sought to avoid the children and grandchildren if we knew they were sick and carried a virus of any kind. Sometimes it fell on birthdays or anniversaries and could not go. With a weak immune system, I would catch the latest bug and become ill. At one time, my blood count was so low that nurses and anyone visiting had to put on a mask and wear a gown. I believe the Good Shepherd watched over me and protected me, just like He said He would. I love to say that the Lord is my Shepherd. Since He is in control of all things, He assures us that His staff will comfort us.

The Mental Obstacles

The next obstacles that survivors face are mental ones. This psychological trauma does not have any physical appearance. DailyMail.com had an article stating; Cancer survivors are

---

[21] (Baertlein)

plagued by symptoms of post-traumatic stress disorder more than a decade after diagnosis according to experts.

Left with psychological scars akin to those inflicted by war, U.S. researchers have discovered that four out of ten cancer patients report lasting behavioral changes. Patients described that years after treatment they were still affected by debilitating symptoms including avoidance, disturbing flashbacks, and depression.

Experts, based their evidence on a survey of 566 patients with non-Hodgkin's lymphoma, a relatively common kind of cancer.

The team from the Duke Cancer Institute in Durham, North Carolina had studied these patients for post-traumatic stress disorder or PTSD symptoms once before, estimating that about one in 12 had full-blown PTSD.
This latest survey reveals how these symptoms often persist.

Post-traumatic stress disorder occurs to 30 percent of people who have experienced a traumatic event.
This can include any situation where a person feels extreme fear or helplessness.

The NHS says someone with PTSD often relives the traumatic event through nightmares and flashbacks.
They may start to avoid situations that remind them of the event or to refuse to talk about it. They may also have problems concentrating and sleeping and may feel emotionally numbed and feel isolated and detached. These symptoms can emerge from hours to months after the event. Doctors may suggest watchful waiting to see if symptoms get worse or improve. Treatments include therapies such as psychotherapy and cognitive-behavioral therapy and medication like

paroxetine. It is just very stressful for people to be told that they have cancer. You cannot just assume that they feel bad now, but it will go away. [22]

Survivors must deal with this kind of mental issues. The mind has a lot to deal with when one considers all the side effects and stress that follow chemotherapy. Any serious illness can impact mental health. Patients, caregivers and their loved ones going through cancer can have a devastating experience. Receiving a potentially fatal diagnosis, going through treatment protocols, and learning to live with limitations can cause depression in many patients, as can side effects from the treatment itself. Managing mental health needs is a crucial part of the treatment process and may even impact prognosis.[23]

We have stress that affects our mind, and on top of all that, is what we call chemo brain. According to the American Cancer Society the exact cause of chemo brain is not always known, and it can happen at any time during cancer, it is also referred to as mental fog.

Though the brain usually recovers over time, the some-times vague, yet distressing mental changes that cancer patients notice, are real, not imagined. They might last a short time, or they might go on for years. These changes can make people unable to go back to their school, work or social activities, or make it so that it takes many mental efforts to do so. Chemo brain affects everyday life for many people, and more research is needed to help prevent and cope with it.

Here are just a few examples of what we call chemo brain: according to the American Cancer Society.

---

[22] (Whitelocks)
[23] (Spiegel)

Forgetting things that they usually have no trouble recalling (memory lapses)

Trouble concentrating (they can't focus on what they're doing, have a short attention span, may "space out")

Trouble remembering details like names, dates, and sometimes larger events.

Trouble multi-tasking, like answering the phone while cooking, without losing track of one task (they are less able to do more than one thing at a time)

Taking longer to finish things (disorganized, slower thinking and processing)

Trouble, remembering common words (unable to find the right words to finish a sentence). [24]

With so much confusion, it's hard to have the proper evaluation of our worthiness. Some come to the conclusion that they are worthless. There is much discouragement that can affect a survivor. How discouraging it can be when it is difficult to do anything, let alone remembering how to do it right. That is why some become bitter and cynical. Their frustration is felt in almost every sentence they make. It is understandable. Some have to give up their independence and look to others for help and support. We need to be sensitive, understanding and encourage rather than criticize. Since we know what goes on, we should be the best friends to lend sympathy and support. By going through different stages of cancer, we can learn to be the best support system available to others.

As survivors, we are educated in an area that healthy people do not have. We must be patient with those that do not understand what cancer is all about. We must not take other

---

[24] (Society, Chemo Brain)

people's expressions too personally when discussing cancer with a healthy person. Many things irritate us because we know differently. The following is a partial list of what has been said to a survivor taken from online:

"It will all be okay, I just know it."
"Someday you will put this all behind you" (to a stage IV patient)
"Don't worry, things will get better." (to a stage IV patient)
"So when will you be all better?" (to a stage IV patient)
"When will your cancer be gone?" (to a stage IV)
"But you don't look sick."
"Lance Armstrong cured his stage IV cancer. You can too."
"But I thought you had chemo and surgery last time. How could it be back? This is why people shouldn't do chemo."
"Do you think it was a waste to do chemo last time?"
"Live in the moment." "Be strong." "Fight hard." "Keep your chin up." "Don't give up." "Attitude is everything."
"We just need a miracle for you."
"If anyone can beat this, you can."
After telling someone, I had Stage IV: "Wow. I'm going to miss you."
 "Is it terminal?"
"What's your prognosis?"
"It could be worse, you know."
"Everything happens for a reason."
"It's all part of a larger plan."
 "You're only given what you can handle."
 "All you need to do is think positive."
 "Half the battle is the mindset. Be determined to beat cancer and you will."

"Now that you've been through this you're due for some good things to happen."

"I'm sure it's fine/I'm sure it's nothing."

"Well, you've been needing a vacation for a while and now [during chemo] you get to lie around and read books all day. What could be better?"

"Well, do they think [the chemo] is going to do any good?"

"At least it is not on your face where everyone could see the scars besides, you don't really need your breasts anyway."[25]

Some of these thoughts are amusing and shows how often people do not think before speaking. I can't expect a healthy person to know and experience the journey of a survivor. I believe we endure experiences to enable us to be better equipped to help someone that crosses our path.

Another mental stress is the recurrent fear factor. Whenever I have a new ache or pain, I wonder if it is cancer-related. I ask myself, is it back? The more often I have a recurrence, the more anxious I am when anything is not going well, or I'm getting sick. Cancer will always be dreaded. I want to overcome the disease, but I'm considered chronic. It will never leave me, but by the Grace of God.

Here is a typical experience with anyone living with the fear factor. One day I had another doctor appointment to receive the results of six months of chemotherapy. I had a PET and a CAT scan, and I was going to get the results. It is nerve wrecking to say the least. One would think that between the time you have a test and get the results, it would be the shortest laps of time possible to make it easier for a patient. Sometimes I don't think Doctors know how we feel when we hear the sound of a bleak report. Of course, they deal with this

---

[25] (Adams)

every day, and they must not let feelings interfere with their profession.

My husband and I usually go to the doctor's office together to hear the results. The fact that everything in nature tends to get worse rather than better leaves us with wonder. Our new cars start deteriorating the day we get it. Our bodies get older and older, and that process isn't getting better even with the advancement of science, but when you add chemotherapy into the mix, you just don't know.

We are all aware there is an end to our lives, but we would like to think we are not yet there. I've asked Claude what his feelings were as we sometimes wait in the doctor's office. I was feeling pretty confident that I would be in remission again. I had peace that all was well.

You do get used to the process after awhile. He felt uncertain of the outcome though looking forward with anticipation to God's grace. We pray every day that we would learn to submit to the will of God. Our motto is taken from the Lord's prayer that He gave us which says "Thy will be done." It is not easy to find God's will sometimes, and not easy to give in to His will. Although when we learn to look to Him, as the Good Shepherd, what is there to worry about? My husband has many plans for us. He always prays that I would go into remission, get to retirement and into retirement in a ministry to reach out and help those that have cancer. We are looking forward in spite of the possible odds.The Bible teaches us to live one day at a time and to walk by faith.

We have often sat in a doctor's office, waiting for results. I am thankful that every time this scenario is before me, I have a loved one beside me to support and encourage. Sometimes my children are with me, to also face an ambiguous report. It is not easy for any of them; it also affects them. So in a doctor's office I need to manage my emotions. By the grace of God, we can become resilient. We can spring back to normal behavior and feelings. Resilient people acknowledge stressful situations, keep calm and evaluate things rationally so they can make a plan and act.

Al Siebert, in his book "The Survivor Personality", writes that "The best survivors spend almost no time, especially in emergencies, getting upset about what has been lost or feeling distressed about things going badly.... For this reason, they do not usually take themselves too seriously and are, therefore, hard to threaten."[26]

On a more humorous note, Patricia Gaffney said: "Bad news doesn't hurt as much if you hear it in good company. It's like, if somebody pushes you out of a 5th floor window and you bounce off an awning, a car roof, and a pile of plastic garbage bags before you smash onto the pavement, you've got a pretty good chance of surviving."[27]

"Always laugh when you can, it is cheap medicine," — Lord Bryon

"I love those who can smile in trouble, can gather strength from distress, and grow brave by reflection," — Leonardo da Vinci

"If my life wasn't funny, then it would just be true, and that is unacceptable," — Carrie Fisher

"Scars remind us of where we have been. They do not have to dictate where we are going."— Unknown

The Good Shepherd helps us in every situation. Sometimes reports are encouraging and other times it can be depressing.

---

[26] (Siebert)
[27]

One time the doctor said the cancer is back in the bag (as he put it), which means that there is no disease activity that they can see! Wow! Good news! How was I to keep this cancer in the bag? There is much discussion on this subject. There are two choices to choose from. Do nothing, till the blood count indicate cancer activity and then get more rounds of chemotherapy, a choice that is becoming harder and harder to endure. Or the alternative is to get maintenance treatments of a lower dose of chemotherapy to ward off cancer cells.

According to a patient education website;

Maintenance therapy is the ongoing use of chemotherapy (the use of drugs to destroy cancer cells) or another treatment to help lower the risk of recurrence after it has disappeared following initial therapy. Maintenance therapy also may be used for patients with advanced cancer (cancer that cannot be cured) to help keep it from growing and spreading further. In either situation, this type of treatment may be given for a long time.

Although the concept of maintenance therapy is not new, it is becoming a more common treatment approach for many different types of cancer. One reason is that new cancer drugs have fewer side effects, and patients may be able to tolerate them longer. Also, new research shows that maintenance therapy can help some patients with cancer delay a recurrence or live longer.

Here are the risks and benefits:

Although maintenance therapy may prevent cancer from returning or slow its growth, there are some possible disadvantages:

- Increased side effects
- Higher treatment costs
- More visits to the doctor or clinic

- Limited data on survival benefit
- Drug resistance (when a drug stops working after prolonged use) [28]

My doctor assures me that the treatments would not make me lose my hair, but it would keep the dormant cells at bay. I now must choose. Choosing is the hardest part, and it adds stress to my life. I want to do the will of God. I want to know where the Good Shepherd is leading me, and follow that path. It takes much thinking and praying to come to the right decision. We need to pray that God touches our hearts and minds so as to lead us in a very particular way.

How does God lead us into making the right decision? We know that He is not going to appear before us and clearly tell us the plan of action to take. If He sent the angel Gabriel to give explicit instructions like He did to the Virgin Mary, it would be easy. You have noticed that it doesn't present itself so easily as that. So, how will we find His will?

There is not a book on planet earth that we can count on as the only truth to live by except the Bible. We do have a promise that He does lead because He is the Shepherd, and we are His sheep. Therefore, on life's journey, how does He lead? We believe that God will use at least four avenues in harmony with each other to lead. They are His Word **the Bible, circumstances, the mind, and the soul.**

We must not choose anything that is in contradiction with His Word. Scriptures acknowledge the importance of a doctor's help and professionalism. Luc 5;31 says: "They that are whole need not a physician, but they that are sick." Circumstances also need to be in harmony and sometimes He uses these things to help us make a decision. We know that finances are often a determining factor in many of our choices.

---

[28] (Board)

For some they just cannot afford certain treatments, so the question is settled. However, because it can be affordable for others, that still does not qualify the mind and the soul. I use the "mind" because I believe that God can use our mind to come to the conclusion about what is the best decision to take when we are praying for His guidance. Yes, God can make us think we do not want to take a particular plan of action, or he can make us believe that we do wish to take a precise plan of action. Prayer is an important tool in finding His leading. When we pray, we must not just consider what would be to our advantage, but consider His will. Remember Jesus's teaching about prayer. He said, when you pray, say **"Thy will be done**."

God can have a plan for someone, and have a different one for someone else. How can that be? It is evident that He did not want everyone to be apostles, not everyone a Noah, or everyone to have the sickness the apostle Paul had, which was given him to make him what he was. Not everyone ends up in jail to testify of God's grace like the apostle Paul or other martyrs. None the less, God can choose to lead someone to be in a particular room to testify of God's grace because that is His plan.

The soul is also a factor to consider when searching God's will. When God leads He also gives peace in the mind or heart. If you don't have peace about something, you should not make a decision. Wait till you have peace in your heart and mind. God wants us to make the best decision based on His Word, His leading, circumstances, and the soul. He can and will lead, and He is the Good Shepherd.

Under the topic, "mental stress and obstacles," there is one more area that I would like to mention. There is the stress of maybe having to leave my children behind when they need me the most. What will they do with out me? What will they remember about me? So many questions and thoughts bombard my mind, concerning them. Questions like, how will they do? How will they get along? What can I do now to make it easier for them when I leave? Why do we have these kinds of feelings? Probably because we are humans, and we have a maternal desire to protect our children and to love them entirely. I am in tune with their lives today, I know what some of their burdens are. I feel for them and often in my condition I cannot help them like I would want. I do help with babysitting, moral support, doing errands, sewing for them. The one thing that counts is what is done for Christ. They know my life, my history, and my failures. My prayer and hope is that they can remember that I did love my Lord, and my desire is to serve Him and that they do the same during their lifetime. We pray every day that they grow in the knowledge of God by studying the Bible. I want my children to be blessed. The blueprint for this blessedness is Psalm 1:

1 Blessed is the man that walketh not in the counsel of the ungodly, nor standeth in the way of sinners, nor sitter in the seat of the scornful.

2 But his delight is in the law of the Lord; and in his law doth he meditate day and night.

3 And he shall be like a tree planted by the rivers of water, that bringeth forth his fruit in his season; his leaf also shall not wither; and whatsoever he doeth shall prosper.

My heart must turn to the one and only who is God. The Shepherd will take care of them like He takes care of us. The total submission into His hands is where He wants us to be. The Good Shepherd says in the New Testament, Matthew 6:34 *"Take therefore no thought for the morrow: for the morrow shall take thought for the things of itself. Sufficient unto the day is the evil thereof."* Though we are prone to worry and be upset about obstacles around us, God wants us to relax through faith in Him. In the world of mystery, it is a comfort to know the God, who knows all things, and takes care of everything. If you look to the Good Shepherd and depend on His guidance, sovereignty, and grace, you will find all you need. This is the good news of Psalms 23 " The Lord is my shepherd," He orders our steps according to His will.

Spiritual Obstacles

The most painful area, to deal with battling cancer is spiritual. I am referring to the part of us, which is invisible, yet affects the mental and physical.

When using the term spiritual, I will not expound on the doctrinal aspect of the Biblical teaching of the Spirit, just to keep it simple and easier to grasp. If we wanted to go into depth, yes, we would see the difference between the soul and the spirit which are both invisible. So the spiritual obstacles are those that tend to block progress in one's life with God. Alternatively, an obstacle is anything that prevents a clear vision of what is before us and what is promised. Our soul needs 20/20 vision when facing the hard times of life. On what do we focus? Do we see only the size of our problems, or do we see the greatness of our God and His plan?

Herbert Vander Lugt gives an illustration of his visit at the hospital with two people that did believe in God. One man was glum and quite listless even when the Scriptures were read and in prayer. His spiritual eyesight seemed dim. When the other man was visited, he found him talking cheerfully with two of his granddaughters. He expressed his desire that they would have a real life, and he urged them to live for Jesus. This man had 20/20 spiritual vision. By faith, he saw the invisible God as he was facing death.

We read of similar responses in Numbers 13 and 14. Twelve spies had been sent out to explore the Promised Land. All 12 saw the lush, green, fertile areas. It was truly a land of high agricultural promise. However, 10 of them were intimidated by the size and number of the hostile people who lived there. They said it would be ridiculous to invade. The other two spies, Joshua, and Caleb insisted that with the Lord on their side they could take the territory. By faith, they saw God beyond the obstacles.[29]

On our journey, there are spiritual obstacles; unbelief, lack of prayer, sin, and lack of direction, all of which can prevent a smooth journey with the Good Shepherd.

1. Unbelief

One spiritual obstacle, which can haunt us and rob us of joy in life, is lack of faith. We need to believe in the one that is leading, and when the contrary happens, we lose the sense of direction. This is like finding oneself in the woods and not knowing how to get out of the forest. Claude tells of his experience in getting lost in the woods. He panicked and even though he came out of the woods in front of the farm that he was looking for, he did not recognize it. He did not realize he

---

[29] (Vander-Lugt)

was at the right place. Fear took over his mind and brought on a terrible feeling.

The first time the cancer word was applied to my account, I felt lost in the woods, wondering how I was going to make it out. We need to grow in faith and we need to feed our soul daily to be in good spiritual health. Our situation as survivors puts us in a frame of mind that wants to know the truth and the words of our Shepherd. If we allow our situation to direct us, it can lead us closer to God and into His Word. Where do we get faith? Romains 10:17 says, "So then faith cometh by hearing, and hearing by the word of God." God can use the trials we go through to draw us to Him and His Word. He can also teach us essential truths. We can find His peace in the midst of our difficulties. So the lack of faith will be a terrible obstacle on our journey. We create the greatest problems in our lives when we neglect Him.

God sometimes plans unexpected routes for His people. We read about one in Exodus 14:10-22. Faced with certain death, either from Pharaoh's army or by drowning, the Israelites were near panic. However, God parted the Red Sea, and they walked through on dry land. Years later, the psalm writer Asaph used this event as evidence of God's mighty power, Psalm 77:19-20 says:
"Thy way is in the sea, and thy path in the great waters and thy footsteps are not known.
Thou leddest thy people like a flock by the hand of Moses and Aaron."

God can create roads where we see only obstacles. When the way seems uncertain, it is good to remember what God has done in the past. He specializes in pathways through all circumstances. He will lead us to paths that point to His love and grace.

2. Lack of prayer

Lack of prayer is another hindrance to anyone's journey through life. What a privilege we have to talk and communicate with the creator of this world. He desires to make our relationship with Him personal, so we can say, **my** Creator, or **my** Lord and **my** Shepherd. He wants us to have an open line of communication for all circumstances at all times. We have a 911 line, always available. I am very thankful for the privilege we have to go to the Lord in prayer.

Facing surgery because of two tumors caused by ovarian cancer, I cried out to Him, and the peace of God came over me. I felt the Shepherd's staff comfort me. We are learning about the importance of looking to Him in every situation of every moment.

Prayer is useful and powerful. There is a hymn that says; "Where can you go, but to the Lord." In the most dangerous and critical moments of my life, I turned to the Lord, and He came to my rescue. He remains the Shepherd, and He will do what He promises in the 23'rd Psalm.

Oswald Chambers wrote: "We tend to use prayer as a last resort, but God wants it to be our first line of defense. We pray when there's nothing else we can do, but God wants us to pray before we do anything at all."

At its root, prayer is simply a conversation with God, spoken in the expectation that God hears and answers. Prayer should not be a last resort. In His Word, God encourages us to engage in prayer (Phil. 4:6). We also have His promise that when "two or three are gathered together" in His name, He will be "there in the midst of them" (Matt. 18:20).

For those who have experienced the power of the Almighty, our first inclination often will be to cry out to Him. Nineteenth-century Pastor Andrew Murray said: "Prayer opens the way for God Himself to do His work in us and through us."[30]

3. Sin.

Sin will keep you from the Bible, or the Bible will keep you from sin. If you want to plunge into worldly pleasures and its riches, then you will be uncomfortable with the reading, teaching, or preaching of the Bible. If God is not Lord, what you have or want is an idol and your god. You should have no other gods before the God of the universe. Those that insist on doing what even the conscience condemns are closing their eyes to the clear leading of the Good Shepherd.

4. Lack of directions.

Who goes anywhere without directions to get there? So you ask. Where are we going? We were born and from observation; we are all going to die. What do we do in between? Where do we get directions? Let us not forget the Good Shepherd has spoken to us and gave us the map, the Old and New Testament, to know what to expect. Would we not take chemotherapy to eradicate cancer cells? Would we not take anti-nausea medicine after chemo to prevent us from getting nauseous? We know that we are the sheep, and He is the Good Shepherd, so why would we neglect instructions from the great physician, the leader, and master? We are referring to the Bible, the very Word of God. Psalm 1 puts it this way,"

---

[30] (Casper)

Blessed is the man that walketh not in the counsel of the ungodly, nor standeth in the way of sinners, nor sitteth in the seat of the scornful. However, his delight is in the law of the Lord, and in his law doth he meditate day and night." We do ourselves a terrible disservice when we neglect His Word. He can only speak to our heart through the road map of the Bible and by the leading of the Holy Spirit. Listen to the master and follow the Good Shepherd.

Notes and thoughts on:
"The Branch."

_____
_____
_____
_____
_____
_____
_____
_____
_____
_____
_____
_____
_____
_____
_____
_____
_____
_____
_____
_____
_____
_____
_____
_____
_____
_____
_____
_____
_____

Chapter 5
"The Bench."

Ps 23: 3 "He restoreth my soul: he leadeth me in the paths of righteousness for his name's sake".

Life is a unique journey for each, that evokes many thoughts from the past and into the future. The bench in the painting was derived from our experience every morning. Early in the morning we would make a fresh pot of coffee, then sit down, and start talking about everything under the sun. However, since the cancer diagnosis, we have been thinking of life and the end of life. The bench represents musings of the important things life has to offer. Oh, what the mortal mind can process when pressured by the evident fear of limited time.

The Brevity of Time

The bench also represents a factor of time set aside for re-flection. There are so many people that leave this world in an instant because of a car accident, airplane crash, or even a heart attack and never had one second to think of getting ready. They found themselves in eternity before God. You would think since death is certain for everyone, people would take time in preparation for the inevitable. Those who receive a terminal diagnose, are suddenly faced with the cold hard fact. Instantly they realize how precious life is. I am thankful my diagnosis caused me to think about the past, the present, and the future. Relative to the shortness of time here below on earth, comes our deepest thoughts of what is important in life.

The journey of our lives is very short in itself. We often neglect to live it to its fullest and can quickly waste the precious time allotted to us. However, with a jolt, we find ourselves sitting on an isolated bench to contemplat the important aspects of life. We are privileged to have the time today. We are not sure about tomorrow. In times of crisis, our sense of what is truly important often comes into clearer focus.

In Psalm 90, "A Prayer of Moses," this man of God looks at life from beginning to end. In the light of the brevity of life (vv.4-6) and the realization of God's righteous anger (vv.7-11), Moses makes a plea to God for understanding: "So teach us to number our days that we may apply our hearts unto wisdom. (v.12). He continues this psalm with an appeal to God's love: "And let the beauty of the Lord our God be upon us and establish thou thy work of our hands upon us; Yea, the work of our hands establish thou it.(v.17)

Threescore years and ten, which is seventy years, give or take a few years, and we are gone (Ps. 90:10). Israel's poet was right: We are but strangers here and sojourners (Ps. 39:12).

The brevity of life should change our lives, even if never diagnosed with cancer. Our days are fleeting.(Ps.39:4). It is a feeling that grows more evident as we draw nearer to the end. We must face the fact that our time here on earth is limited.

We are not alone on the journey. Since God is with us, it makes the journey less troubling, less frightening, less worrisome. We pass through this world and into the next with a loving Father as our constant companion and guide. We are strangers here on earth, but we are never alone on the journey (Psalm 73:23-24). We have the Shepherd who says, "I am with you always" (Matt. 28:20).

We may not have the presence of a father, a mother, a spouse, or friends, but we always know that God is walking beside us. An old saying puts it like this: "Good company on the road makes the way to seem lighter."[31]

Here are some quotes of those that have already gone, shortly after they pondered the brevity of life.

"When we fully understand the brevity of life, its fleeting joys, and unavoidable pains; when we accept the facts that all men and women are approaching an inevitable doom: the consciousness of it should make us more kindly and considerate of each other. This feeling should make men and women use their best efforts to help their fellow travelers on the road, to make the path brighter and easier as we journey on. It should bring a closer kinship, a better understanding, and a deeper sympathy for the wayfarers who must live a common life and die a common death."

---

[31] (Roper)

— Clarence Darrow, The Essential Words and Writings of Clarence Darrow

"It is not that we have so little time but that we lose so much. ... The life we receive is not short, but we make it so; we are not ill provided but use what we have wastefully."
— Seneca, On the Shortness of Life

"As humans, we do not like to think about our own immortality. We are not interested in speaking in terms of there not being a tomorrow. Rather, we speak as if things will continue on in the future as things have continued in the past. However, deep down inside of us, we do realize that anything can happen to us at any given moment. We have seen and perhaps experienced the sudden loss of life of family members and friends. There are horror stories of family members lost due to drunk driving. Nightly local news reports of people doing that which they would do every day, but this time dying in car accidents, shootings, or some other unforeseen event."[32]

The Bible says it this way:
James 4:14-16
" *Whereas ye know not what shall be on the morrow. For what is your life? It is even a vapour, that appeareth for a little time, and then vanisheth away. For that, ye ought to say, If the Lord will, we shall live, and do this, or that. But now ye rejoice in your boastings: all such rejoicing is evil.*"

Since time is of the essence, we need to consider the future and the impact or effect it will have on those in our lives. We

---

[32] (Kercheville)

need to consider our children and the preparation of our last will and testament. Since I have a good idea of what lies ahead of me, I want to prepare my children for the inevitable. I'm sure they are wondering how I am taking it personally. They can tell by my attitude and my demeanor. I am handling it pretty well, only because I believe in the Good Shepherd.

If I can lead my children to having a positive attitude concerning the hand that is dealt them, the happier they will be. We all have to deal with problems and hardships and tribulations. However, if we have the right attitude because of the one we believe in, then, we will be the happiest. I already lost my father and mother. My husband lost his father, and his mother is 90 years old this year. It is not easy to lose anyone. We have a strong hope that we will see all of them one day in the presence of God. All others who have accepted Jesus Christ as their personal savior are sure to be there also. Faith in Him helps us live a better life, with priorities in harmony with the Word of God. As we ponder the thought of leaving this world, maybe sooner than later, we are left with a profound truth, life is precious.

Since, we have time to reflect on matters that concern us, what about taking the time to heal from within. Since cancer strikes the healthy and the unhealthy alike, we often wonder, where does it come from? Bad things happen to good people and vice versa. I certainly do not blame God or myself for the situation I am in. However, I can say in retrospect, there are things I wish never happened. I have failed in certain areas of my life. Some things I can repair and others, it is too late. Cancer can lead a person to this kind of thinking. There is a book entitled **"Don't Waste Your Cancer."** On the eve of his cancer surgery, John Piper writes about cancer as an opportunity to glorify God. With pastoral sensitivity, compassion, and strength, Piper gently, but firmly, acknowledges that we can indeed waste our cancer when we don't see how it is God's good plan for us and a hope-filled path for making much of Jesus.

I found that cancer helped me understand how to love myself and others. There are many things sometimes that you must let go of and let God take over. Forgiving myself and others is crucial. When love is manifested towards others, it brings the greatest happiness. It is amazing what can be done with a life that is stricken with sickness.

Charles Spurgeon once said, "Health is a gift from God, but sickness is a gift greater still." Throughout his time in this world, Spurgeon suffered from various physical ailments that eventually took his life prematurely. He longed to be well, but he recognized the supreme value of being sick, and he thanked God for it because it was his pain that caused him to draw near to God desperately.

Joni Eareckson Tada says, "My wheelchair was the key to seeing all this happen—especially since God's power always shows up best in weakness. So here I sit … glad that I have not been healed on the outside but pleased that I have been healed from the inside. I have been healed from my own self-centered wants and wishes."[33]

"Breast cancer always happened to other women, not me," says Joni Eareckson Tada. "Forty-five years of living in a wheelchair provided enough challenges, without thinking of cancer." All that changed in June 2010 when Joni was diagnosed with stage 3 breast cancer. Yet Joni's attitude never changed. She continues to reach out and live and share the love of God in her life. All her books and seminars improve

[33] (Tada)

the lives of millions. None of this could have happened if she had been well all her life.

Our thoughts about reaching out to others are because of my cancer. It started by wanting to have a website to help people find financial sources, encouragement, links to find anything they would need. ***HopeThroughCancer.com*** was the result and the name we came up with, for internet users. Before I knew it, I was sewing for others making rag quilts; my husband started oil painting. Then we were making gift baskets giving them away free of charge. We started attending a support group and it led us to writing this book. I do believe it took cancer in my life to direct us where we are today. We have found much satisfaction in touching lives and encouraging others.

We have learned to be servants to others while serving our God. It occupies our minds, and we do things that are beneficial to us and others. Here is a list of what some survivors have done after being diagnosed with cancer.

-Dedicated money for research
-Volunteer work at cancer organizations
-Raised money for research
-Walked for cancer research
-Ran for cancer survivors
-Invented products
-Wrote books
-Served on committees to help survivors
-Made speeches to encourage survivors
-Visited survivors at hospitals
-Made oil paintings
-Sewed rag quilts for survivors in chemotherapy
-Sewed different articles for survivors

-Brianna Commerford, 14, says she is a "normal kid" again, back to school in Washington Township, NJ, hanging out with her friends and participating in gymnastics and competitive cheerleading. However, Brianna is also extraordinary. Since completing her treatment for Hodgkin lymphoma, she has become a national spokesperson for childhood cancer, spoken before the US Congress about a bill to help develop new childhood cancer treatments, and helped raise more than $30,000 for the American Cancer Society. [34]

I have come to the conclusion that cancer is not all about me. I had to understand that my cancer affected those around me, my husband, my children, co-workers, and friends. People that are sensitive also hurt for those they care about. Let's think about them for a couple of minutes.

The Spouse

In a marriage, when cancer strikes one of the spouses, the other becomes the caregiver. They are affected in so many ways that everything is like cancer to them. Their emotions are torn, and depression can also set in. Life changes for them like it does for the patient. While I am now living with everything about cancer, like chemotherapy, doctor visits, blood tests, results of scans, so does the spouse. The caregivers take time off work, and go to the doctor's office. They sit on pins and needles awaiting the results also. They deal with the bad news and try to encourage the ill spouse as best they can.

Their life has changed dramatically. Work now is in retrospect to an added financial burden. Everyone knows that

---

[34] (Commerford)

it can be devastating to couples because of added financial pressure.

As if a cancer diagnosis wasn't taxing enough on a family, a new study confirms what many cancer survivors have experienced firsthand: Having a cancer diagnosis can lead to to financial difficulties. Statistics are not encouraging in this area.

Whatever a situation spirals into concerning finances, a solution can be found. Some cancer patients have it easier than others. Some live in a country that might have social medicine and the cost does not affect them. Here in the United States with our health system as it is can be difficult. The Good Shepherd's promises do not change because of where you live or if a problem is greater. He is the same and will lead to feed and care for His own. There is not a situation that He cannot find a solution to.

We have learned to count on Him for all things. He does and will provide during physical and financial burdens. Under much strain and sickness, the one to look to is the one that provides the light on our path. Cancer.net has put together a comprehensive list of organizations that offer help, including grants for medical costs, travel and housing. Sometimes the solution is not even found in organizations. God is not limited to anything. He sometimes provides in miraculous ways. He wants us to look to Him and He provides like He has promised to do.

Those that have so much money and are not affected by the high cost of cancer treatments are not the majority. The important fact of the matter is to learn to rely not on ourselves but on God.

The spouse also has to deal with the emotions of the patient. Sadness is a terrible feeling that the husband or wife must face. Couples usually are in tune how the other feels. If there is something wrong, the other one can sense it. The problem the patient has is that he or she is dealing with all kinds of side effects and fear concerning cancer. The caregiver that has a close relationship with the spouse can suffer similar feelings. After a while, there is a strong possibility that this affects the relationship. Real love is put to the test when one of the spouses is diagnosed with cancer. The relationship is strained because activity, outings, trips, restaurants, intimacy, are often put "on hold" to allow the cancer patient to heal.

Dr. Marc Chamberlain, director of neuro-oncology at the Seattle Cancer Care Alliance and one of the authors of the Cancer study says: "The majority of husbands take excellent care of their partners, but men, on the whole, tend to be less comfortable doing so." Chamberlain adds that the demands of a spouse's illness can interfere with one's ability to earn a living, which may be harder for men to swallow -- or afford.

And these days, notes Jimmie Holland, M.D., a psycho-oncologist at Memorial Sloan-Kettering Cancer Center in New York, caregivers fill a larger role than ever: "In the past, a person would stay in the hospital for weeks. Now people come home with wounds that need to be cleaned, and all kinds of other things we once used to think only nurses could do."

This difficult job grows even tougher in the absence of emotional support. While women turn to friends, counselors, or groups for the help they need, men don't. A man typically relies on his spouse as his main confidant, and when that spouse is sick, he can find himself in a downward spiral of isolation. "You can end up with an alienated individual," says Louise Knight, a social worker at Johns Hopkins Kimmel Cancer Center. "He doesn't have anyone to hang on to."

An article by Donna Jackson Nakazawa says: So what distinguishes the couples who do make it through? After hearing from many people across the country about their need for support—and their disappointment in discovering that so little help exists—she decided to find still married couples and talk to them about how they make it work. While the specifics varied, she discovered that, for the most part, the successful couples weren't dealing with fewer or easier problems. But each of them was somehow able to use the challenges to strengthen their relationship rather than weaken it—often in ways that would benefit any marriage.[35]

How can a caregiver and a spouse with cancer succeed as a couple in such difficult situations? The answer is not in becoming a statistic like everyone else. Disaster was not meant to separate but can be an instrument to draw together. Hope is the answer. Having hope in the Good Shepherd's words, the Bible.

When the spiritual part of man is healthy and strong, he or she can face the most difficult adversities. Opposition like cancer quickens the spiritual part of a human being. Tribulation seems to be a growth factor in life. Those that follow the Good Shepherd are not exempt from these things, but when faced are able to overcome hardship. They draw their strength from God who understands, cares and leads to maturity. Couples often draw closer to each other, and their love grows.

When love grows stronger and stronger through the grace of God and His Word, commitment to each other as a couple, strengthens greatly. The caregiver serves and helps the spouse the best way known to comfort and bring happiness.

---

[35] (Nakazawa)

Satisfaction and joy is a reward that comes by doing acts of love to make the patient happy in spite of the diagnosis.

The hope of success and happiness is promised to those that follow the Good Shepherd. It has been said that the couple that prays together stays together. We can also say the couple that reads God's Word stay together. Those that obey His Word have victory together though stricken with cancer. Happiness, unity, joy, and care are attainable even when on a journey with cancer when God is the center of it all.

The bench in the painting represents time spent reflecting on so many things that can be overwhelming. The spouse must be considered, so, may God bless that husband or wife who gives "from the heart" to lighten the load of the other. Here is the test of love. Love gives and does not expect in return. How can a sick person have the best attitude and disposition all the time? Can the spouse expect that from a patient? It would not be reasonable, but love, in spite of sickness or health, is crucial.

We have made the best of our situation by finding a common goal, mutual interest, following and serving the Good Shepherd the best we know how. We look out for each other and understand each other, we look to others in the same situation as survivors and caretakers.

The Children

The second subject I want to mention, is children. They are of concern because of the stress they experience. All parents want to protect their children from the pain that life can bring. Although it is not possible to control the reality of having cancer, it is possible to make a real difference in how your children handle the experience and go on with their lives after you are gone. According to "The American Cancer Society," Patients with terminal cancer often worry that this experience will destroy their children's ability to enjoy life in the future. Health care experts who have worked with many families dealing with cancer say that this is rarely the case. In fact, children can and do go on to live normal lives even with the impact of a parent's illness and the loss they go through when a parent dies. This may be hard to believe, but most children, with the help of family and others, learn to be happy again and enjoy their lives. It may give you strength to know you can affect how your children feel about your illness and how well they can move beyond it in the months to come.

Remember that your experience with cancer is only one part of your child's life. Unless your kids are very young, there have probably been many years in which you were not sick. If your children are very young, the memories of your illness will fade into the background. Having a parent with cancer is only one part of your child's development and does not, by itself, lead to lasting damage to them as adults. The essence of parenting is to love your children and help them feel secure. You can continue to do this in spite of the stresses that cancer may cause you and your family.[36]

The following paragraphs gives an insight of what a child can think and feel when a parent has cancer. My son Jamie put it this way.

"I can remember exactly where I was and what I was doing on 9/11/2001 after the first plane crashed into the twin towers. I was working, doing lawn service and I was running a weed eater and I can show you the house I was working on. I don't remember if it was a Monday or Friday, but I remember that

---

[36] (Society, Dealing With A Parents Terminal Illness)

everything seemed to stop and nothing really mattered except that we just got attacked. Feeling helpless and vulnerable and not knowing what this all meant for my family and myself.

Well, that is exactly how I felt when my Mom called me to tell me that she had ovarian cancer. I don't remember the day, but I can tell you exactly where I was. I was driving down Federal Hwy just south of Atlantic Ave. It felt like the world literally stopped and nothing else really seemed to matter. A feeling of panic and fear set in. Is she going to die, is this something that can be cured? I had so many questions that I wanted answers to and at that time there were no answers. I have known people who have had cancer. My Grandfather and Grandmother both died of cancer, but when I heard the news about them I was sad, but I cannot tell you where I was or what I was doing. It did not affect me the same. When it is your Mom and she is young, I really don't have words to describe what I felt.

When we got the news, I was 4 years sober. In my sobriety, I had learned to rely on God and accept life on life's terms. That's easy when life is going well and with only minor bumps in the road. This was no little bump, this was a sinkhole that seemed too big to handle. I prayed shortly after I hung up the phone with Mom and asked God to, please help me to not freak out and think the worst. With a lot of prayers I was able to take it one day at a time until we knew what we needed to do.

I remember the day we all went to the oncologist to find out the course of action. The whole family was there and the doctor told us he would have to perform a major surgery to remove the cancer. That was on a Friday and the following Tuesday we were all at the hospital waiting for the results. It was one of the longest days I can remember. Finally, the doctor came down to the waiting room to tell us the outcome. He proceeded to tell us everything they had to remove. I asked him point blank, is it terminal? He looked at me and said if this were 5 years ago I would have closed her up and told you there is nothing we can do, but with the progress with chemotherapy she had a chance. I don't remember exactly what the percentages were, but the bottom line was she could have 5 years if we were lucky. That was 7 years ago.

As my Mom was going through chemotherapy I would visit her every Tuesday and whenever else I could. It is not easy watching someone you love being so sick, but, my Mom kept a smile on her face and cracked jokes and stayed positive. I can only hope that if I ever have to go through cancer that I can go through it with the faith, courage, and perseverance that she did. She has been an example to me of how a person with faith acts and lives and I am grateful for that.

Some people feel the need to blame God when things like this happen. I did not blame God at all. I do not think God gives cancer, I think cancer is a part of life and some get it and some don't. I would pray every day and ask God to give my Mom comfort and the strength she needed to get through this. I would ask God to take care of her, whether it was in heaven or here on earth, and asked Him not to let her suffer. I asked God every day to help me accept whatever happened and to trust it was His will. My mother, going through cancer, really taught me what faith in God was all about. I didn't know what the outcome was going to be, but I was o.k. with whatever happened.

My "Mom" having cancer brought my family closer together and it taught me to spend as much time as I can with

the people I love because you never know when those people
will be gone.

When we found out, my Mom had cancer, she had 1
grandchild who was 14 years old. Now 6 years later she has 4
more. Emma 4, Gavin 4, Sayge 17 months, and Abbie 3
months. Our family is strong, and Mom is the matriarch. I am
so grateful that God's will was to have her stay with us
because I cannot imagine our lives without her. Every time she
has a recurrence and has to go through chemo again, it is
scary. We are faced with reality, but, we keep putting one foot
in front of the other to walk through whatever is in front of
us."

The bottom line, when thinking of all that concerns us, we
must not worry, like the Bible commands us to do. Our
children will have the Good Shepherd also if they give their
life to Him. Maybe seeing our hope in Him will influence their
lives to follow the Lord also. Hearing our children say from
their heart, "the Lord is my shepherd," would surely ease our
pain concerning their lives without us. When I ponder what
has happened in the last six years, I am thankful. Despite
cancer, I appreciate the beauty of life and the way the
Shepherd has led me in the valleys and the mountain tops. The
journey has been peaceful and revealing. I would not want it
any other way!

Last Will And Testament

Another important subject to consider at the bench, so to
speak, is to get the estate in order since it is time sensitive and
becomes pressing and significant. You should prepare your
last will and testament and or trust fund. While trust funds, or

trusts, may seem the province of the wealthy, there are actually many benefits to creating them, even if you're not a multimillionaire. Trusts can help you manage your property and assets, make sure they are distributed after your death according to your wishes, and save your family money, time, and paperwork.

Simply put, a trust is a legal document established by an individual or corporation known as a grantor. The trust holds property or assets for a particular person or group, called the beneficiary. Control of the trust is maintained by a trustee -- in some cases the grantor is the trustee, and in others the grantor names a trusted family member, friend or professional.

There are many reasons to set up a trust, including avoiding probate, providing for your family after your death, and stating exactly how, and when, your descendants receive their inheritance. But not everyone should establish a trust -- for some, a standard will is a better choice. Although do-it-yourself kits are available, the applicable laws are complicated, and anyone considering a trust should consult a lawyer.[37]

Avoid Probate

One good reason to have a trust fund often cited as a key reason for establishing a trust, avoiding probate can mean substantial savings in time, legal fees and paperwork. If your assets and property are to be distributed according to your will, probate is the process by which a judge determines the will's validity. A trust allows your descendants to bypass this process and gain access to the assets and property more

---

[37] (Cassidy, Finances)

quickly. Plus, your family can avoid probate fees, which can be as much as 5 percent of your value. The probate process is also a long one, and can take up to a year or even two to finalize, during which time your family can't touch their inheritance.[38]

Minimize Conflict

Another good reason a trust is necessary is because trusts can minimize possible conflict between heirs when an estate is being settled. They are highly customizable, allowing grantors to tailor the document to the needs of their situations. A grantor can detail the exact items and monetary amounts to be left to each beneficiary. This is particularly helpful when dividing items that heirs may argue over, or items that may have sentimental value. A grantor can decide to leave, for example, a painting to a child who particularly appreciated it, a piece of furniture to a relative who is a collector and a car to a grandchild who admired it. With all of the specifics spelled out, heirs have little reason to argue over "who gets what." Trusts offer more control than wills in complex family situations, such as when leaving assets to a married beneficiary. Unlike a will, a trust can be customized so that a beneficiary's spouse cannot gain access to the inheritance without the beneficiary's consent.[39]

Privacy

One last good reason to have a trust is because they offer greater privacy than wills because "trusts" do not go through

---

[38] (Nolo)
[39] (Cassidy, Finances)

probate, so there usually aren't any public records of them. This means your assets and whom you leave them to are kept private.

Notes and thoughts on:
"The Bench."

_____

_____

_____

_____

_____

_____

_____

_____

_____

_____

_____

_____

_____

_____

_____

_____

_____

_____

_____

_____

_____

_____

_____

_____

_____

_____

_____

Chapter 6
"The Still Waters."

*Ps 23:2   "He maketh me to lie down in green pastures: **He leadeth me beside the still waters."***

As we follow the Good Shepherd through life, in every area, we are given the best that life has to offer. We often hear it said, that grass is greener on the other side of the fence. That is not the case in green pastures where the Lord leads. There is no better place! You may be tempted to think that it is better because of what you see. However, only God can direct to the best places for your soul and happiness. The comparison with the sheep and the pastures and the still water is significant. We are introduced to what the body needs and what our soul thirst for. Since we are compared to sheep in this psalm, the pastures represent the place for nourishment required to survive. We have nothing to worry about since He feeds the sparrows every day, and we are worth much more to Him than the sparrows.

The Shepherd directs His sheep into situations that eliminate fear and want. Green pastures for sheep are best for them. In rough terrain, where grass is sparse, sheep will eat almost to the root of the lawn. Alternatively, they can eat leaves and the bark of shrubs. Green pastures provide tender grass to eat and a cool spot to lie on. It is a good place for dwelling and quiet rest, even in the noon heat and dryness. We are not just tempted to imagine a perfect setting of satisfaction, we are led there to be satisfied.

Remember that sheep are representative of God's children. Left to themselves they cannot find such lush, green, cool grass to meet their needs. Unless they are brought there by His grace and love, they will wander away according to their own inclinations. The Good Shepherd leads us to the best place. The one who leads is personal. He will deal with us in a way that we are close to Him, and feel loved. You can talk to computers and animals, but there is no personal touch. The Lord wants to deal with us in such a way that we can say, "The Lord is **my** shepherd." God is a Shepherd that leads individuals. David said, "the Lord is **my** shepherd." It is as if David were saying that he knew the God of the universe was personal to him and in control, as the Good Shepherd, for his whole life. Do you know that? Do you know the Lord as your Shepherd like David did? According to David and his knowledge, he lacked nothing. Some versions say, "The Lord is my shepherd, I have everything I need." Like a Good Shepherd, God gives Himself to us and for this reason, we lack nothing. The rest of verses 2-4 only bear this out. How can we fail to trust a God who has so willingly made Himself available to us?[40]

We read in the same verse that He will provide and lead. A commentary explains the provisions this way. We see, in verse 2, that God's provision is perfect. David says that a good shepherd leads his sheep to green pastures and quiet waters. The green pastures probably refer to the tender young shoots that grow up in the morning and are loved by the wildlife of Palestine. The calm waters probably refer to a well-spring with fresh water. The psalmist wants us to understand that this Shepherd goes all out for his sheep. The Shepherd wants them to have the best and is likewise sensitive to their needs. David wants us to understand that God does the same for His people. It was David's experience, and it ought to be ours. Some of us have deep struggles with our present financial or job situation as well as other things. However, we need to come to grips with the truth, that as we seek God, we are not getting second best from Him. He is a faithful Shepherd to give us only what is excellent according to His purpose and agenda. Can you trust Him for that? Listen to what Paul said:

"He who did not spare His own Son, but delivered Him up for all of us, will He not then, along with Him, graciously give us all things" (Romans 8:32).[41]

Notice that he leads to still waters. You have probably been close to a raging river that is flowing with such force and might that it is scary to think of falling into it and being carried away. Imagine being in front of Niagara Falls. Just looking at the immensity of the fall is scary. The drop at the falls is about 160 feet. More than 168,000 cubic meters (6

---

[40] Bible.org

[41] (Bible.org, Psalm 23)

million cubic ft.) of water go over the crest line of the Falls every minute during peak daytime tourist hours. It attracts tourists because of its beauty, but it is a frightful scene. It is dangerous, and you can feel it and see it. If life were always on the brink of a waterfall, it would be horrible.

Sheep are much like humans in the sense they are scared of the noise and rushing water. They like calm still waters. They enjoy a peaceful environment. So the Good Shepherd leads them to a place where they find calmness and rest.

A great preacher said: What are these "still waters" but the influences and graces of his blessed Spirit? His Spirit attends us in various operations, like waters—in the plural—to cleanse, to refresh, to fertilize, to cherish. They are "still waters," for the Holy Ghost loves peace and sounds no trumpet of ostentation in his operations. He may flow into our soul, but not into our neighbor's, and, therefore, our neighbor may not perceive the divine presence; and though the blessed Spirit may be pouring his floods into one heart, yet he that sitteth next to the favored one may know nothing of it.[42]

If we grasp the message of this psalm, and the mental picture of a shepherd and his sheep, we would do well to seek Him first, in all things. Can He help the children that have cancer? Is He leading us in spite of cancer? He will always be the Shepherd that leads us to calm waters. What do "the still waters" represent in our state of battle? It signifies two things.

1.Peace

Since cancer has been a part of my life, I have faced many scary moments and panic feelings of reality. By the grace of

---

[42] (Spurgeon, The Treasury Of David)

God, I have learned to turn to God and accept what I have and every time I have called out to Him, He has given me peace in my soul. We hear about the peace with God and the peace of God. The two go together, yet you can not have the peace of God without having peace with God. What the world gives compared to God's peace, is vaslty divergent. What can the world give? Well meaning people try to give false hope and peace by saying, don't worry everything will be okay. They often believe a lie, thinking peace can be found in success, prosperity, positive experiences, or individual relationships. However, the only source of lasting tranquility is found in the presence of Jesus. What the world has to offer will crumble under pressure. However, God's peace can carry His people through every hardship. The world provides no assurance for the body that aches and no certitude for the soul in eternity. John 14:27 says, "Peace I leave with you, my peace I give unto you: not as the world giveth, give I unto you. Let not your heart be troubled, neither let it be afraid."

The Holman Bible Dictionary defines peace as a "sense of well-being and fulfillment that comes from God and is dependent on His presence." Rather than expressing an absence of stress or conflict, the Hebrew word shalom, and the Greek indicate the presence of peace, health, restoration, salvation, and reconciliation with the Lord.

The peace with God is due to the gift of salvation. A gift that is received through the acknowledgment of having sinned and being in need of a savior, because there is no way to save oneself by works, good deeds, attitude or anything else. We must realize we cannot earn or win anything from God through our efforts. We must either receive or refuse it as a gift. God died on the cross of Calvary and bore the condemnation of our sins by Himself on our behalf so that we might be saved from an eternal hell.

John 3:16-17 says:

16 For God so loved the world, that he gave his only begotten Son, that whosoever believeth in him should not perish, but have everlasting life.

17 For God sent not his Son into the world to condemn the world; but that the world through him might be saved.

All who have accepted Him as personal Savior, have peace with God. We have a Shepherd to lead us. Condemnation of our sins no longer exists. We have been pardoned, washed whiter than snow, and have a sure place reserved in heaven for eternity. We have been saved by God's love manifested on the cross of Calvary and offered to all those that believe. To believe is more than just to know. The majority of the world knows that Jesus was crucified. History affirms such a fact. However, few accept that He was God and man's Savior. I accepted Jesus as my personal Savior when I was ten years old and Claude was twelve when he accepted Him. We have had the peace **with** God ever since. The peace with God, which is accomplished forever puts us in a non-changing status. This does not mean that we have experienced the peace **of** God all through our life. The peace of God depends on our walk with God.

We have a beautiful promise in Philippians 4:7, that says: *"And the peace of God, which passes all understanding, shall keep your hearts and minds through Christ Jesus."*

Even though we know God as our Savior and we meditate on His Word and feed our minds on those treasures, we can miss out on the peace of God. We quickly lose peace of mind and soul over trivial things and certainly over major problems.

Sometimes it is an insignificant matter that takes away our peace, like dust in the eye, which can cause great distress. We are such feeble creatures that we quickly lose our peace of mind just with a word or a look! It is hard for the sea of our heart to remain a long time in a smooth and glassy state—it may be rippled and ruffled by an infant's cry. As a survivor, it does not take much to jump on the bandwagon and lose the peace we so earnestly need. What about the doctor's visit tomorrow? Or the results of a blood test? Alternatively, when we feel something abnormal we relentlessly associate it with a return of cancer or even worse, the end stage of the disease.

Our hearts and soul are easily agitated when we are on the verge of panic, due to the sure end results of cancer. We can know that our eternity is settled, yet, we may lose the peace of God in our hearts. It is like facing dangerous waterfalls instead of enjoying the calm still waters. The Good Shepherd wants us to enjoy what He has provided and where He has led us. If a sheep closes its eyes and imagines itself before a raging waterfall, it will stay in a state of terror. If the sheep opens its eyes and sees the still waters, it will be calm and happy to be there to drink and be refreshed.

It is interesting to see that the Shepherd uses still waters as a symbol of calmness. A report explains that since ancient times, humans have assigned healing and transformational properties to water. In early Rome, baths were an important part of cultural life, a place where citizens went to find relaxation and to connect with others in a calm setting. In Ayurveda, the ancient Indian medicinal wisdom and traditional Chinese medicine, the water element is crucial to balancing the body and creating physical harmony. Rivers have long been seen as sacred places, and in some different spiritual contexts, water has symbolized rebirth, spiritual cleansing, and salvation.

Today, we still turn to water for calmness and clarity. We spend our vacations on the beach or at the lake; get exercise and enjoyment from water sports like surfing, scuba diving, sailing, and swimming. We refresh ourselves with long showers and soothing baths and often build our lives and homes around bodies of water. Wallace J. Nichols, a marine biologist, believes that we all have a "blue mind" as he puts it, "a mildly meditative state characterized by calm, peacefulness, unity, and a sense of general happiness and satisfaction with life at the moment" -- that's triggered when we're in or near water. He also says: "We are beginning to learn that our brains are hardwired to react positively to water and that being near it can calm and connect us, increase innovation and insight, and even heal what's broken."

The Shepherd brings us to these still waters on our journey, but maybe we have not opened our eyes to see where we are. When we see through faith, and trust the promises given to us, only then do we feel the ambiance of still and calm waters. The work of the Holy Spirit allows us to see with the eyes of our heart even if our bodily eyes are blinded. A great preacher said it this way:

"Your heart is troubled and though you are believing in Christ for salvation and are, for this reason, safe, yet for all that, your inward rest may be broken. Therefore would I turn the text into a prayer and pray for myself and every believer in Jesus Christ—that the peace of God which passes all understanding may now keep our hearts and minds through Christ Jesus. May you all know the text by experience. He who wrote it had felt it—may we who read it feel it, too. Paul often enjoyed the brightness of peace in the darkness of a dungeon,

and he felt living peace in the prospect of a sudden and cruel death. He loved peace, preached peace, lived in peace, died in peace and, behold, he has entered into the fruition of peace and dwells in peace before the Throne of God!"[43]

It is beyond human understanding that a person could be stricken with cancer or some other disaster in his or her life and still find, peace like a still river. This peace passes all understanding. For this reason, those that experience this beautiful gift will be amazed and shocked. I felt this peace when I was on a stretcher facing a major operation. The possibility of death was on the table. I was leaving behind life as I knew it, and saw tears in the eyes of my husband and children. However, I found the peace of God. I cried out to Him, and His peace came over my heart and soul. I was at the still waters that He promised. I was like on fire but not burning inside. I was drinking the cool refreshing still waters. I was falling but only into His hand. That is where I was because the Good Shepherd was with me. I must realize that the Word of God is real. I probably would have never felt it this way, if it were not for the fact I got cancer. My relationship with God has become a way of life. Now I know this is the only way to live and to be happy here on planet earth. I know with such certitude what the still waters are like, so, I pray for those that are not at peace at this moment. Cry out to Him now. He will hear and give you the peace that He alone can give.

Open your heart to Him, believe His promise and you will experience the peace of God as if you are lying down in cool pastures beside the still waters. I like the illustration presented by a renowned preacher; "We may talk about inward rest and

---

[43] (Spurgeon, The Peace Of God)

dilate upon the peace of God. We may select the most choice expressions to declare the delicacy of its enjoyment, but we cannot convey to others the knowledge second hand—they must feel it or they can not understand it. If I were speaking to little children, I would illustrate my point by the story of the boy at one of our mission stations which had a piece of the sugar cube given him one day at school.

He had never tasted such essence of sweetness, and when he went home to his father, he told him that he had eaten something that was wonderfully sweet. His father said, "Was it as sweet as such-and-such a fruit?" "It was far sweeter than that." "Was it as sweet as such-and-such food?" that he mentioned. "It was much sweeter than that. But Father," he said, "I cannot explain it." He rushed out of the house back to the mission house, begged for a piece of sugar and brought it back. He then said, "Father, taste and see, and then you will know how sweet it is." So I venture to use that simple illustration and say, "O taste and see that the peace of God is good," for in very deed it surpasses all the tongues of men and angels to set it forth!"[44]

2.The Word Of God

The still waters, represent the peace of God, and also His Word. We know we have symbols that represent all God can do in a spiritual and physical world. He does not want us to lack anything, in the world we live. What does the water represent? What are these "still waters" but the influences and graces of His blessed Spirit? His Spirit attends to us in various operations, like waters, in the plural, to cleanse, refresh, strengthen, and cherish. The word of God is all that to the

---

[44] (Spurgeon, The Peace Of God)

heart of a Christian. In the Psalm the Shepherd leads sheep to green pastures and still waters. The typical activity would be to approach and drink. His sheep follow and are led by Him. The activity of the Christian should be to go to the Holy Scriptures, read and meditate to receive the blessings and inspiration it gives. It is fitting that we are only led to the water. We are not forced to drink; we are compelled but not obliged to drink. It is one thing to want to drink fresh water when there is none, and it is another thing to not drink when you are at the right place for perfect satisfaction. Many Christians going through hard times with health issues do not find peace because they do not go to the source and drink.

According to "Christianity Today" a research found that 80% of Churchgoers do not read the Bible daily, LifeWay Survey Suggests.

According to RNS, (Religion News Service), More than half of Americans think the Bible has too little influence on a culture they see in moral decline. Yet, only one in five Americans read the Bible on a regular basis, according to a new survey. If they do read it, the majority (57 percent) only read their Bibles four times a year or less. Only 26 percent of Americans said they read their Bible on a regular basis (four or more times a week). Younger people also seem to be moving away from the Bible. A majority (57 percent) of those ages 18-28 read their Bibles less than three times a year if at all.

The survey showed, that the Bible is still firmly rooted in American soil: 88 percent of respondents said they own a Bible, 80 percent think the Bible is sacred, 61 percent wish they read the Bible more, and the average household has 4.4 Bibles.[45]

---

[45] (Bell)

The statistics "about reading the Bible" should not be the influencing factor for you or me. We get up early in the morning every day. We have our coffee and then we read the Bible. Reading is also accompanied by devotional books. After reading, we get on our knees, and pray for health, our grandchildren, our children, siblings, ministries we support, and for those that have cancer or are sick. We pray for those that preach the Word of God. There are so many areas that we cannot control, so we present them at the throne of grace, into the hands of the Good Shepherd. We are relieved that God is greater than circumstances and He can override any situation. We are thankful that He hears and answers our prayers in His time.

Here is what the Scriptures says about those that read and meditate the Holy Scriptures.

Psalm 1:2 *"But his delight is in the law of the LORD, and in his law doth he meditate day and night.*

Joshua 1:8 says:
"This book of the law shall not depart out of thy mouth; but thou shalt meditate therein day and night, that thou mayest observe to do according to all that is written therein: for then thou shalt make thy way prosperous, and then thou shalt have good success."

Psalm 119:97-99
97 "O how love I thy law! It is my meditation all the day."
98 "Thou through thy commandments hast made me wiser than mine enemies: for they are ever with me."
99 "I have more understanding than all my teachers: for thy testimonies are my meditation."

1 John 5:3 *"For this is the love of God, that we keep his commandments: and his commandments are not grievous."*

The still waters in the painting also represent a truth in the Bible, which is the same in nature. Tree growth and water is a picture of spiritual maturity and is compared to meditating the Word of God. Beautiful trees bending over the river bring beauty and shade to harsh summer days. We become like a tree planted by the rivers of water. As we grow, we produce fruit, and become spiritually healthy. We are happy, satisfied and feel the presence and guidance of our God. We become examples of those that follow the Good Shepherd.
The Bible says in the first Psalm, verse 1-3:

1 Blessed is the man that walketh not in the counsel of the ungodly, nor standeth in the way of sinners, nor sitteth in the seat of the scornful.

2 But his delight is in the law of the Lord; and in his law doth he meditate day and night.

3 And he shall be like a tree planted by the rivers of water, that bringeth forth his fruit in his season; his leaf also shall not wither; and whatsoever he doeth shall prosper.

To grow into such a description, is to be planted by water, so the roots can get the water needed. The water is to be absorbed. Though the sheep are led to still waters, they must drink to satisfy thirst and the body's needs. It is not enough to look and admire the color or the clarity of the water. Unless it is absorbed, there will be no benefits which is also true for the believer. Unless God's Word is meditated, there is no other way to know how to live and what to believe. If the Bible only accumulates dust, it will serve no purpose.

The truth about being fruitful and mature is an important subject to consider. Again the rivers of water are compared to the Word of God or the Law of the Lord. If the Word of God is not found and meditated, the end result is disastrous. The Good Shepherd leads beside still waters and wants His child happy, prosperous, fruitful, and beautiful. We need to be as strong as a mighty oak planted by the river.

The comparison of a man to a tree is frequent in the Book of Job and occurs once in the Pentateuch (Numbers 24:6). We find it again in Psalm 92:12-14 and frequently in the prophets. His strength and fruit depend on the irrigation and the proximity to the water. There will be nothing lacking "in God's provision" to be happy and fruitful, for the believer who takes the time to read and meditate God's Word.

Notes and thoughts on:
"The Still Waters."

Chapter 7
"The Light."

Ps 23:5 Thou preparest a table before me in the presence of mine enemies: thou anointest my head with oil; my cup runneth over.

Religion and astronomy may not overlap often, but a new NASA X-ray image captures a celestial object that resembles the "Hand of God."

In his devotion, Dennis Fisher brings out this wonder. When NASA began using a new kind of space telescope to capture different spectrums of light, researchers were surprised at one of the photos. It shows what looks like fingers, a thumb, and an open palm showered with spectacular colors of blue, purple, green, and gold. Some have called it **"The Hand of God."**

The idea of God reaching out His hand to help us in our time of need is a central theme of Scripture. In Psalm 63 we read: "Because You have been my help, therefore in the shadow of Your wings I will rejoice. My soul follows close behind You; Your right hand upholds me" (vv.7-8). The psalmist felt God's divine help like a hand of support. Some Bible teachers believe that King David wrote this psalm in the wilderness of Judah during the terrible time of his son Absalom's rebellion. Absalom had conspired to dethrone his father, and David fled to the wilderness (2 Sam. 15–16). Even during this difficult time, God was present and David trusted in Him. He said, "Because your loving-kindness is better than life, my lips shall praise You" (Ps. 63:3). Life can be painful at times, yet God offers His comforting hand in the midst of it. We are not beyond His reach.[46]

In Chapter 7, the artist focuses on the "light" that shines through the trees and illuminates the path depicted as our life's journey. To see the path clearly, the Good Shepherd who is the "Light of the World" needs to be known to each of us in a personal way. He will then be able to enlighten us and lead us along the way.

The Good Shepherd is also the light of the world. John the Baptist was a witness that Jesus, the light of the world, was the true light, and we should be His witnesses too.
John 1:6-9 says:

6. There was a man sent from God, whose name was John.

---

[46] (Fisher)

7. The same came for a witness, to bear witness of the Light, that all men through him might believe.

8. He was not that Light but was sent to bear witness of that Light.

9. That was the true Light, which lighteth every man that cometh into the world.

John 8:12 says; *Then spake Jesus again unto them, saying, I am the light of the world: he that followeth me shall not walk in darkness, but shall have the light of life.*

John 12:35-36 says:

35. Then Jesus said unto them, Yet a little while is the light with you. Walk while ye have the light, lest darkness come upon you: for he that walketh in darkness knoweth not whither He goeth.

36. While ye have light, believe in the light, that ye may be the children of light. These things spake Jesus, and departed, and did hide himself from them.

The Holy Word of God, "the Bible" is also looked upon as light for our path.

Psalm119:105 *Thy word is a lamp unto my feet, and **a light unto my path.***

We read in Psalm 23 *that He leads in the **paths of righteousness.***

His Word and He as a person are inseparable. John 1:1-2 says: *In the beginning was the Word, and the Word was with God, and the Word was God.*

Every morning before day break, my husband and I, sit in a quiet place, engage in conversation around the Word of God. The sun shines in on us, in our peaceful setting, overlooking the gardens. It reminds us of God's light and love filling our hearts and souls. He reveals Himself through the reading and meditation of His Word. The light in the oil painting symbolizes God's revelation and His presence. Meditating on His Word is a start to loving life, knowing His leading and accepting the plans for each of us. His ways are perfect, full of blessings

One of the greatest treasures man has ever received from God is His revelation. It is true that through, "nature" He manifests His intelligent design. His creation of surpassing magnificence, intricately work together in perfect harmony and timing. He performs wonders that cannot be fathomed, like the continuous movement of water between the earth and the atmosphere, revolving planets and moons, the complexities of the human body and mind. He calls His creation "good" seven times in the first chapter of Genesis. Seven is the Biblical number for perfection. If you pass sunlight through a prism, it produces seven colors - three primary colors and four secondary ones. In the realm of Minerals and Geochemistry, there are seven crystal systems. Even the Periodic Table of the known Elements appears to have seven levels of periodicity. We have seven days in a week.

The following is an excerpt from Bullinger's book: BULLINGER, E. W., "NUMBER IN SCRIPTURE", The Lamp Press, London, 1952.

The Number 7

PHYSIOLOGY offers a vast field for illustration, but, here again, the grand impress is seen to be the number **SEVEN**. The days of man's years are "Three-score years and ten" (7 x

10). In SEVEN years the whole structure of his body changes: and we are all familiar with "the seven ages of man".

The various periods of GESTATION (pregnancy) also are commonly a multiple of SEVEN, either of days or weeks.

With INSECTS, the ova are hatched from SEVEN half-days (such as the wasp, bee, etc.); while, with others, it is SEVEN whole days. The majority of insects require from 14 (2 x 7) to 42 (6 x 7) days; the same applies to the larva state.

With ANIMALS the period of gestation of:

The mouse is 21 (3 x 7) days.
The hare and rat, 28 (4 x 7) days.
The cat, 56 (8 x 7) days.
The dog, 63 (9 x 7) days.
The lion, 98 (14 x 7) days.
The sheep, 147 (21 x 7) days.

With BIRDS, the incubation of:
The common hen is 21 (3 x 7) days.
The duck, 28 (4 x 7) days.
With the HUMAN species, it is 280 days (or 40 x 7). [47]

Renowned scientists, such as ISAAC NEWTON, who contributed so much to modern physics and mathematics, spent many years of their personal research on the subject of "Numerics in the Bible". Newton must have felt that he was "onto something". Seven is also seen throughout the Bible.

---

[47] (E.W.Bullinger)

Why? Because, God is the maker of both of them. Jesus and the Bible are forever linked. They are, in reality, the same thing. He is truly the Word of God. The title, "the Word", given to Jesus, is found 7 times in 5 verses, including being found in 1 John 5:7 (also see John 1:1; 1:14; 1 John 1:1; and Rev. 19:13)!

Here are a few examples where the number 7 is found in the Bible. It will suffice to take Michael Hoggard's article in the introduction to God's divine number. The number 7 is God's very own number and is associated with Divine completion and perfection. It becomes apparent to most who read the Scriptures that the number 7 is the most significant number in all of the Scriptures. Therefore, it stands to reason there must be some extremely important patterns that are associated with the number 7.

The entire Bible is based on the things that God Almighty has said to His servants, the prophets. They wrote these things down exactly as they had received them. That is why the Bible is such a perfect book. It comes from a perfect God. A common phrase that is found in the Old Testament, "Thus saith the Lord of Hosts", is a phrase that reveals to us that God has indeed given us the very words that have come directly from His mouth. This phrase is found exactly 70 (7 x 10) times in the King James Bible.

The phrase, "his servants the prophets", is found 7 times in the Bible (see 2 Kings 17:23; 21:10; 24:2; Jeremiah. 25:4; Dan. 9:10; Amos 3:7; and Rev. 10:7). Notice that in, Amos and Revelation the Lord chose to place it in the 7th verse so that we would know that it has a special meaning. In each case, we find that the prophets are the recipients of the Word of God.

The Bible is a book of prophecy. The word "prophecy" is found 21 (7 x 3) times in the Scriptures. The 21st occurrence of this word reveals that we should be very cautious about how we handle the Word of God: "And if any man shall take away from the words of the book of this prophecy, God shall take away his part out of the book of life, and out of the holy city, and from the things which are written in this book" (Revelation 22:19).

The very first version of the written "Word of God" was the Ten Commandments. God has placed a very important value on the Ten Commandments, for we find them located in the 70th chapter of the Bible, Exodus 20. The Bible mentions that they were written on "tables of stone". In fact, the Bible mentions 14 (7 x 2) times that they are written on "tables of stone". Also, in the 70th chapter of the New Testament (John 2), you will find the very first miracle that Jesus performed.
It is clear that the words, phrases, verses, chapters, and books of the Bible have been arranged in a perfect order. It would be impossible for men to manipulate a group of documents in this manner, especially men who, in many cases, lived thousands of years apart. How do we know which "Word of God" to use? We are told that Jesus is the Word of God in John 1:1. In 1 John 5:7 He is also given that title: "For there are three that bear record in heaven, the Father, the Word, and the Holy Ghost: and these three are one." It seems odd that most modern translations omit verse 7 or place a note by it that says this passage does not appear in some Greek texts! This phrase is found exactly 49 times (7 x 7) in the Authorized Version of the Bible! [48]

---

[48] (Hoggart)

The Bible is the road map for life and especially on the dark paths of adversity. The Good Shepherd tells us that His sheep follow Him. We get to know the Shepherd by His Word given to us. We have one of the greatest gifts to man, the Bible.

The Bible is the Word of God.

"How do you know that the Bible is the Word of God?" is a frequently asked question. The Bible is unique among "Holy Books." It is rooted in and intertwined with actual human history. The Bible claims to be "the Word of God." It records the interaction of God with historical people and nations. It reveals the meaning of life and the responsibility of human beings to their Creator. The Bible is actually a collection of books, some long, some short. This book of books is the world's all-time best seller and the world's most translated book.

Michael Houdmann in his article "Is The Bible Truly God's Word?" presents both **internal** and **external** evidence that prove the Bible is truly God's Word.

Internal Evidence

The **internal** evidence is those things within the Bible that testify of its divine origin. One of the first internal evidences is seen in its unity. Even though it is sixty-six individual books, written on three continents, in three different languages, over a period of approximately 1500 years, by more than 40 authors who came from many walks of life, the Bible remains one unified book from beginning to end without contradiction. This unity is unique from all other books and is evidence of the divine origin of the words which God moved men to record.

Internal evidence that indicate the Bible is truly God's Word is the prophecies contained within its pages. The Bible contains hundreds of detailed prophecies relating to the future of individual nations including Israel, certain cities, and mankind. Other prophecies concern the coming of one who would be the Messiah, the Savior of all who would believe in Him. Unlike the prophecies found in other religious books or by men such as Nostradamus, biblical prophecies are extremely detailed. There are over three hundred prophecies concerning Jesus Christ in the Old Testament. Not only was it foretold where He would be born and His lineage, but also how He would die and that He would rise again. There simply is no logical way to explain the fulfilled prophecies in the Bible other than by divine origin. There is no other religious book with the extent or type of predictive prophecy that the Bible contains.

A third **internal** evidence of the divine origin of the Bible is its unique authority and power. While this evidence is more subjective than the first two, it is no less a powerful testimony of the divine origin of the Bible. The Bible's authority is unlike any other book ever written. This authority and power is best seen in the way countless lives have been transformed by the supernatural power of God's Word. Drug addicts have been cured by it, homosexuals set free by it, derelicts and deadbeats transformed by it, hardened criminals reformed by it, sinners rebuked by it, and hate turned to love by it. The Bible does possess a dynamic and transforming power that is only possible because it is truly God's Word.

External Evidence

There are also **external** evidences that indicate the Bible is truly the Word of God. One is the historicity of the Bible. Because the Bible details historical events, its truthfulness and accuracy are subject to verification like any other historical document. Through both archeological evidences and other writings, the historical accounts of the Bible have been proven time and time again to be accurate and true. In fact, all the archeological and manuscript evidence supporting the Bible makes it the best-documented book from the ancient world. The fact that the Bible accurately and truthfully records historically verifiable events is a great indication of its truthfulness when dealing with religious subjects and doctrines and helps substantiate its claim to be the very Word of God.

Another, **external** evidence, that the Bible is "truly" God's Word, is the integrity of its human authors. As mentioned earlier, God used men from many walks of life to record His words. In studying the lives of these men, we find them to be honest and sincere. The fact that they were willing to die often excruciating deaths for what they believed testifies that these ordinary yet honest men actually believed God had spoken to them. The men who wrote the New Testament and many hundreds of other believers (1 Corinthians 15:6) knew the truth of their message because they had seen and spent time with Jesus Christ after He had risen from the dead. Seeing the risen Christ had a tremendous impact on them. They went from hiding in fear to being willing to die for the message God had revealed to them. Their lives and deaths testify to the fact that the Bible truly is God's Word.

One, final external evidence that the Bible is truly God's Word, is the indestructibility of the Bible. Because of its importance and claim to be the very Word of God, the Bible has suffered more vicious attacks and attempts to destroy it than any other book in history. From early Roman Emperors like Diocletian, through communist dictators and on to modern-day atheists and agnostics, the Bible has withstood and outlasted all of its attackers and is still today the most widely published book in the world.[49]

Therefore, the God of the universe keeps His Word and gives us nothing but satisfaction. He promises to prepare a table in the presence of enemies. His promise of the provision is twofold, food for the body and food for the soul. The food for the soul is always the word of God. The enemy is twofold, the enemy of the body and the enemy of the soul. No matter what comes our way, God will provide every need. We can say with confidence and joy, "I shall not want."

"The anointing of the head with oil" is a picture of God giving an abundance of good things, not only for necessity, but for pleasure and delight. God's abundance fills us with spiritual joy and comfort. His giving is always plentiful. The words "**my cup runneth over**" are an expression of an over-flowing bountiful supply.

Everything received from the Good Shepherd is like a picture of light falling from heaven with its warmth and revealing qualities. Light and the Word of God have similar qualities. Both will purify. The Word of God will purify our thoughts and lives. It reveals who we are and who God is. He knows us better than we know ourselves. He is the Creator of heaven and earth. Just as there is beauty in light, seeing the colors of light separated by a prism, so is the beauty of His Word when revealed.

---

[49] (Houdmann)

The comforting and inspirational truths discovered while reading and meditating the Bible help me accept the path and journey I must walk. His Words are a lamp and a light on my path with cancer.

Light is necessary to purify, reveal or illuminate. It has a positive effect on the mind. According to Marcus Felicetti, sunlight has several healing benefits. Sunlight was used for injured soldiers to disinfect and heal wounds. The sun converts high cholesterol in the blood into steroid hormones and the sex hormones we need for reproduction. In the absence of sunlight, the opposite happens; substances convert to cholesterol. Medical literature published in Europe showed that people with atherosclerosis (hardened arteries) improved with sun exposure. It also enhances the body's capacity to deliver oxygen to the tissues; very similar to the effects of exercise. The sun has a great effect on stamina, fitness, and muscular development. The noon sunshine can deliver 100,000 lux. When we sit in offices for the best part of the day, out of the sun, under neon and artificial lights (150-600 lux), we are depriving ourselves of the illumination of nature. Sunlight deprivation can cause a condition called seasonal affective disorder (SAD), a form of depression. It is more common in winter months, but also common in people who work long hours in office buildings.[50]

When I consider the life of a blind person like Fanny Crosby, it is clear that it is not what we have in life as far as possessions and health that makes a beautiful life. It is not cancer that stops anything either. She could not see with her natural eyes, but she could see with her heart. She could not explain what a human face looked like, but she knew the face of God.

---

[50] (Felicetti)

Blind from six weeks old because of a surgical mishap, her life was different than most, but it was not worse than most. Fanny Crosby (1820-1915) supported herself as a teacher at a blind school, she had dear and close friends around the world, and she wrote and published thousands of beautiful hymns, many that are still sung today. Regarding her plight in life she wrote the following words:

"It seemed intended by the blessed providence of God that I should be blind all my life, and I thank Him for the dispensation. If perfect earthly sight were offered me tomorrow, I would not accept it. I might not have sung hymns to the praise of God if I had been distracted by the beautiful and interesting things about me."

The light that comes from the Good Shepherd will do all these things in the mental and spiritual areas of our life. He has been with me, gives me assurance and peace while on the journey. But He also promises an eternity with Him in a perfect environment!

Notes and thoughts on:
"The Light."

Chapter 8
"The Bridge."

Our journey through life has many bridges, and eventually there is one last bridge to cross. Every experience of life shapes and molds us into who we are today. There is nothing we have to fear when we walk with the Good Shepherd. The Psalm reminds us that:

"Yea, though I walk through the valley of the shadow of death, I will fear no evil: for thou art with me."

In life, there are also many rivers to cross but with a bridge the crossing is much easier. The Shepherd is there at every crossing. Sometimes He carries us through the deep waters. One thing is sure. Every river is crossable with the help of the Lord. In the artist's perception of the journey, the bridge is in the background representing experiences in life. Accompanied by the light of God, we have guidance and victory for every problem we face.

It is often said, "I will cross that bridge when I get there." Where did that expression come from? Wikipedia says that this expression is an English-language proverb that is rich in metaphor. When taken literally, it does not make sense but has meaning as a proverb. "Cross the bridge" is a metaphor for solving a problem or overcoming an obstacle. "Until you come" to the bridge is a metaphor for waiting until a vague or low-probability problem arises so you can learn more about what the problem is, before trying to solve or overcome it. The following sentences paraphrase various aspects of the proverb:

1."Wait for ill-defined problems to be clarified before dealing with them."

2."Don't be concerned about distant-future problems until they become near-present problems."

3."Don't try to solve that problem until you are prepared to deal with it."

4." Don't waste your time preparing for all potential problems, because most of them will no longer be problems when you get to them, or because conditions will have changed by then."

5."Don't work on that problem until the scheduled time." [51]

We can be thankful that we do not have to deal with any problem before us even if we perceive there is one, or we fore-see some. Each day presents new challenges. Every day, as well as our tomorrows, are in God's hands and He leads us in the paths of righteousness. In this chapter, we are going to make reference to the two bridges: the bridge of challenges and the last bridge.

---

[51] (Wikipedia)

The Bridge of Challenges.

The bridge of difficulties is very common to cancer survivors. I am prone to look far ahead, and get worked up over things that might never happen. I feel that every day is precious time given to me to live at my best. I cannot live my life to its fullest if I am bogged down with cares of tomorrow. When there is a bridge to cross, I want to be successful making the crossing. Often, you and I encounter struggles and difficulties that require good decision-making skills to overcome. We are tempted to give up on those sick days filled with terrible aches and pain that seem unbearable. The excellent news is that we are not alone, trying to persevere. The Good Shepherd is holding us close, sometimes even carrying us in His arms. He is our comfort and strength during our times of trouble. Oh, may I never forget, I am not alone. The journey is with the Good Shepherd. The task seems easier now that I live with not only the thought of His presence, but with His presence.

Are you tempted to give up? Can you find the courage and strength to carry on? There is hope and encouragement available by putting your complete trust in the God who loves you dearly. He walks with you all the way.

M.Farouk Radian, introducing his book says: *It is now clear that depression is a state of loss of hope that a person reaches after discovering that his efforts are yielding no results. The right way to become enthusiastic once again even while you are depressed lies in two words, finding hope.*[52]

---

[52] (Radwan)

Hope in the Good Shepherd will keep you going and enjoying life and blessings. As survivors, we have many challenges ahead of us. Here are just a few of them listed.

Deteriorating health

Aches and pain

Recurrences of cancer

Loss of hair

Nausea

Maintenance treatments

Financial burden: Co-pays,

    Out of pocket (Insurance)

    Hospitals

Fear of viruses

Strengthening the immune system

Holding on to hope

The best way to face these and be encouraged "through it all" is to take one day at a time. Not one day at a time in your strength and power, but in the power of the Lord. The Scriptures say in Philippians 4:13, *"I can do all things through Christ, which strengtheneth me."*

Focus your attention on the Shepherd and you will be amazed at the courage and hope that follows faith in Him. The message of this book is to give hope through cancer or in any other trial in your life. My sincere prayer is that you will draw closer to the One who loves you more than words can express. May you trust in Him for your life and future, and strength for your daily walk, until the moment you cross the last bridge.

The Last Bridge

The last bridge is the one that transitions us from this side of the world to the next world. The end of this bridge is eternity. By now you know that I believe that we exist in a spiritual world, even when death occurs. The subject of death needs to be dealt with sensitivity and care. We do not want to think that far ahead. It is hard to grasp and face the fact that we will die, and death is the last bridge to cross.

Let's take a few minutes to face it together and see what to expect. You probably have never thought of death as it will be explained in this last chapter. Many do not even let children visit funeral homes because they try to hide the cold hard fact that even they will die at an appointed time.

Unless you believe what God has revealed in the Bible about death, it is difficult to discuss death. No other sources of information exist that are more worthy of our attention as the Holy Scripture. What does it say? Do you know what it means? Are you sure of what it means? Death is an emotionally difficult thing to face. It breaks our heart to lose a loved one. Do you get that feeling of panic when you think of this happening to you? Knowing the truth and trusting the Lord can eradicate apprehensive feelings.

The Good Shepherd definitely knows how we struggle with the thought of dying. He deals with the subject, in the 23rd Psalm. Death is a natural process of life. "Dying" was the result of man's disobedience to God's will. We all have an appointed time to die. The dictionary puts it in a blunt way. *To die is to cease to live; undergo the complete and permanent cessation of all vital functions; become dead.* However, according to the truths of the Bible, it is not as bad as it seems. Having cancer appears to put us close to the inevitable. We have to deal with this every day. We need to know what is ahead in that area. The Psalm says: *"Yea, though I walk through the valley of the shadow of death, I will fear no evil: for thou art with me."*

God's presence is with each believer, as promised throughout the New Testament. The Holy Spirit takes residence in our hearts and communes with us every day of our life. Believers are never alone. Communion with Him and meditating on Him will build our faith in a tangible way as we grasp for the real things that are unseen.

A meditation journal illustrates God's presence with twenty-year-old Lygon Stevens, an experienced mountaineer who had reached the summits of Mt. McKinley, Mt. Rainier, four Andean peaks in Ecuador, and 39 of Colorado's highest mountains. "I climb because I love the mountains," she said, "and I meet God there." In January 2008, Lygon died in an avalanche while climbing Little Bear Peak in southern Colorado with her brother Nicklis, who survived. When her parents discovered her journals, they were deeply moved by the intimacy of her walk with Christ. "Always a shining light for Him," her mother said, "Lygon experienced a depth and honesty in her relationship with the Lord, which even seasoned veterans of faith long to have." In Lygon's final journal entry, written from her tent 3 days before the avalanche, she said: "God is good, and He has a plan for our lives that is greater and more blessed than the lives we pick out for ourselves, and I am so thankful about that. Thank You, Lord, for bringing me this far and to this place. I leave the rest—my future—in those same hands and say thank You." Lygon echoed these words from the Psalmist: "My help comes from the Lord, who made heaven and earth" (Ps. 121:2). [53]

---

[53] (McCasland)

Psalm 23 says; we have the presence of God when we walk through the shadow of death. Is there really such a VALLEY of the SHADOW of DEATH? Or is this something to be taken figuratively or as a metaphor representing the trials, tribulations and sorrows of life? According to Sandy Bruce, there really is such a place. So WHERE was it, or is it? It is along the road going down from Jerusalem towards Jericho, which is located in the Jordan River Valley. It is still there today. It is a steep, winding road, with rocks and a huge cliff on the right side. Shepherds would walk in the deep valley below, in order to get from one place to another. Thieves and bandits could hide along the top of the hill, by the road, or in crevices along the slopes of the hills. Looking down, they would wait for shepherds to pass through, and attack them and steal their sheep. This is the location of the teaching by Jesus about the "Good Samaritan" in Luke 10:25-37. "A certain man went down from Jerusalem to Jericho, and fell among thieves, who stripped him of his clothing, wounded him, and departed, leaving him half dead { in the shadow of death }. " (Luke 10:30) Understanding that the VALLEY of the SHADOW of DEATH was a real place, a real road -- often used by those going from Jerusalem to Jericho -- gives us a better understanding of what Jesus was talking about.[54]

The valley of the shadow of death mentioned in the Psalm is either a place or an experience. Going through a dangerous valley exposes one to hurt, loss, and sometimes even death. But whether a physical place or emotional experience, the trust must be put in the leadership and presence of the Shepherd.

---

[54] (Bruce)

The reference is still to the shepherd. Though I, as one of the flock, should walk through the most dismal valley, in the dead of the night, exposed to pitfalls, precipices, devouring beasts, etc., I should fear no evil under the guidance and protection of such a Shepherd. He knows all the passes, dangerous defiles, hidden pits, and abrupt precipices in the way; and he will guide me around, about, and through them. The idea is that of death casting his gloomy shadow over that valley - the valley of the dead. Hence, the word is applicable to any path of gloom or sadness; any scene of trouble or sorrow; any dark and dangerous way. Thus understood, it is applicable not merely to death itself - though it embraces that, but to any or all the dark, the dangerous, and the gloomy paths which we tread in life: to ways of sadness, solitude, and sorrow. All along those paths God will be a safe and certain guide.[55]

It appears that the valley of the shadow of death consists of the danger and the process of death. This psalm has been read over and over again at funerals, inferring that death no longer has a shadow because life is no longer there. What can be very concerning and scary, is the thought of death or the possibility of death. The shadow of death is not as bad as it is dreaded, with a child of God. Through this valley or rocky ravine, the heavenly footman has to follow the path appointed for him in God's eternal purpose. Spurgeon said it this way: *Gloom, danger, mystery—these three all vanish when faith lights up her heavenly lamp, trimmed with the golden oil of the promise.*

The description of death is described, as a shadow. A shadow leaves gloom over the person involved, but the shadow will not injure and destroy. A shadow may startle you at the

---

[55] (C. Commentary)

moment, but there is nothing there. A sword cannot fight off a shadow, any more than we can destroy death. Death is here to stay, but death will not destroy those that are in Christ. John Bunyan in his book "The Pilgrim's Progress" represents the pilgrim as putting up his sword when he came into the Valley of the Shadow of Death. He had fought Apollyon with it, but when he came into the midnight of that horrible valley, it was of no use to him. Everything was so veiled, magnified and blackened in the dark. I Corinthians 15: 55-57 says *"O death, where is thy sting? O grave, where is thy victory? The sting of death is sin, and the strength of sin is the law. But thanks be to God, which giveth us the victory through our Lord Jesus Christ."*

In this Psalm, David, is described as being calm, assured, and confident. His calmness is due to the one that is with him. He is with the Good Shepherd. If God is for us, who can be against us? God stays with us through every situation of life's journey. To be in danger, or to feel and see shadows of danger, is to be usually afraid of what may happen. Most people would be frightened on their deathbed. This was not the case with David, who portrays assurance and confidence even before the possibility of death. God did not intend only to spend eternity with His sheep, but to stay with them till the end.

Barnes comments on "For thou are with me" explains it as: *Thou wilt be with me. Though invisible, thou wilt attend me. I shall not go alone; I shall not be alone. The psalmist felt assured that if God was with him he had nothing to dread there. God would be his companion, his comforter, his protector, his guide. How applicable is this to death! The dying man seems to go into the dark valley alone. His friends accompany him as far as they can, and then they must give him the parting hand. They cheer him with their voice until he becomes deaf to all sounds; they cheer him with their looks until his eye becomes dim, and he can see no more; they cheer him with the fond embrace until he becomes insensible to every expression of earthly affection, and then he seems to be alone. But the dying believer is not alone. His savior God is with him in that valley, and will never leave him. Upon His arm he can lean, and by His presence he will be comforted until he emerges from the gloom into the bright world beyond. All that is needful to dissipate the terrors of the valley of death is to be able to say, "Thou art with me." [56]*

May God help us to grasp the reality and the truth that God is with us? God is the creator of everything. We do not deserve to look even upwards to Him. Yet he promises to accompany us all through life.

Death eventually comes to all of us. For the Christian, the dark door of death is to be viewed as only a shadow. As frightening as death may appear, the other side, is the bright and shining gate that leads to life eternal with Jesus!

Author William H. Ridgeway recalls that when he was a boy, he and his friends would pick berries. After filling their baskets, they would wait beside a nearby railroad track. As the sun was sinking in the west, a train would come by and "run over them." Of course, the iron monster with its thundering noise and screaming whistle didn't actually run over them at all. It was only the shadow that passed over them. There they sat, knowing there was no danger but shivering in anticipation at the approaching locomotive and box cars. As the train swept by them, they were in its shadow for just a few moments and then it was gone. The setting sun bathed them in a golden

---

[56] (B. Commentary)

glow as they walked to the inviting warmth of home. What an excellent illustration of what it means, for Christians to "walk through the valley of the shadow of death" (Psalm 23:4).

What is the moment of death like? No one has ever come back to talk to us about it except the Lord himself who says" I will be with you." We have heard of many that had a near death experience and many times those that explain it, do not talk as if it was a bad experience. Many talk about the tunnel and the light at the other end. You may have read or heard about many who have died and seen heaven for them- selves. They describe such a realm that is beyond descrip- tion. Some who died and came back to life have said they have seen their lost loved ones in heaven, their family, friends, and some even their pets. This is difficult to prove, yet the sheer number of those who have seen heaven and came back from death is hard to refute; only they themselves know this for certain. But the Bible does describe some of what heaven is like in the scriptures. It is, from the human standpoint, in- describable (I Cor. 2:9).[57]

The first thought that flashes by in your mind about heaven is probably tiny chubby angels playing their harps, because that is how the media presents it. Most people hardly have a clue what heaven will be like. God will be there and that is the extent of their best imagination.

What Will Heaven Be Like?

Without exhausting the subject, we will look to the Bible to give us an idea of what heaven will be like. There are facts

---

[57] (Wellman)

that are evident and taught in the Bible that can clarify the truths about heaven. How can we long for heaven if we do not have a real comprehension of heaven? Can we desire a place that we do not have any idea about? Why is it, heaven is not preached in the pulpits to the extent of Biblical teaching? The same truth is applied when we talk about Hell. Many never get ready for eternity because they don't know or fear what hell would be like. If they knew how it was, they would do everything in their power to never step foot in hell. Jesus talked more about hell than He did about heaven. He warned mankind of its reality. The fact of hell is not preached and probably because preachers don't want to offend and scare people about it. We will concentrate some time on heaven because that will be the eternal home to those who believe in the one and only Savior, Jesus Christ.

The Bible plainly declares that we all deserve hell, a lost eternity, separated from God. But, this changes for a believer because the price of sin and our hell was paid by the One who died on the cross of Calvary for us. So heaven is given to those that are saved from hell, and who are believers in Christ Jesus.

To discuss heaven, we will look at four areas by answering the following questions.
1. What will we be like?
2. Where will we be?
3. Who will we see there?
4. What will we do there?

What will we be like?

It is important to understand our identity and, therefore, appreciate the place we will be for eternity. According to the

Bible, it is sufficient to say we will be the same as we are to-day, without a body and without fallen human nature. However, and at the same time, we will have a form that we can describe as an intermediate body while we await the resurrection. Believers can be assured they will have a visible form or an intermediate body. During the transfiguration scene in Matthew 17, Moses and Elijah appeared, in their intermediate bodies and the disciples were able to recognize them in their physical form. At the resurrection, we will receive an incorruptible body forever, a body without cancer or disease, and one that will never die.

Many seem to have the idea that at death, they become someone new, not knowing where they came from, or who they used to be. That is not what the Bible teaches. In Luke 16: 19-31, the text concerns the rich man and Lazarus who both died. After death, one was consoled because he was a believer. The rich man was tormented in a place called hades. Those that are lost in Hades are conscious, have their memory, their faculties, feelings, and have knowledge of the past life.

The Lord Jesus gives this as an accurate account of two people that died. The Lord does not provide examples that were not real facts. Lazarus is described as being carried by the angels into Abraham's bosom. This was a place where believers went until the resurrection of Christ. Now they go directly to heaven. The apostle Paul said in 2 Corinthians 5:8, *"We are confident, I say, and willing rather to be absent from the body, and to be present with the Lord."*

When we die, we will have our memory. We will remember the things that happened to us on planet earth. We will remember the truths we were taught about Jesus. We will remember life as we know it today. We will be who we are now, without a corrupt body or fallen nature. When those two things are taken away, there is no physical pain, nor evil temptations ever to deal with again. What a deliverance that will be!

A good example of memory from the past life is found in Revelation 6:10, *"And they cried with a loud voice, saying, How long, O Lord, holy and true, dost thou not judge and avenge our blood on them that dwell on the earth?"*

These martyrs were asking God, when would He, revenge and show justice to those on earth that had shed their blood or taken their lives? These believers knew how they died. You will remember your death and your life. We will still know about our children, our life, and our loved ones.

The comforting truth is that we will see everything in a different way. There will be no more hatred, shame, sin, revenge, wrong attitude, sinful nature, selfish seeking motives, or jealousy. We will be happy and we will give God the glory for all that He has done. We will praise His attributes, His justice, His power, His knowledge. Every time we glorify God, the angels will probably join in and we will hear trumpets and singing with praises. There will be no more tears, sorrow, shame, remorse, or sadness. Revelations 24:4 says, *"And God shall wipe away all tears from their eyes; and there shall be no more death, neither sorrow nor crying, neither shall there be any more pain: for the former things are passed away."*

A commentary says; we now have a natural body, but then we will have a spiritual body. This probably doesn't mean that we will be like ghosts floating around unable to interact with things around us. After all, I Corinthians15:49 declares we will have a body like Jesus's resurrected body. And Jesus, after His resurrection, told them to touch Him and to watch Him eat, demonstrating that He was not merely a spirit (Luke 24:37-43). It's more likely that as the natural body is fitted for this present life in our physical universe, the spiritual body will be that which will best suit us for the eternal existence. We will be equipped for our eternal abode. Jesus's resurrected body was capable of entering locked rooms at will (John 20:19). Our earthly body limits us in ways (and/or dimensions) that our spiritual body will not.

We are not told exactly what we will look like in the next life, or what age we will appear to have. But, while many believe we will bear some resemblance to what we look like now, we do know that in whatever ways our appearance or health has been altered as a result of sin, these traits will not be carried over into the next life. More importantly, the sin nature, inherited from Adam (Romans 5:12) will no longer be with us, for we will be made after the holiness of Christ (1 John 3:2).[58]

It seems clear that we will not have gender differences in heaven though our memories of who was male and female on earth would not be forgotten. I believe we will know who our spouse on earth was. However, it will not make a difference because there is no marriage in heaven.

The Sadducees in Jesus's days wanted to trick Jesus with a question about a woman that had seven husbands. They asked Him what husband would she have in Heaven? Jesus answered in Matthew 22:29-30, *"Jesus answered and said unto them, Ye do err, not knowing the scriptures, nor the power of God. For in the resurrection they neither marry, nor are given in marriage, but are as the angels of God in heaven."*

Our greatest relationship will be with God. We will need nothing else but Him. If you have experienced the joys and blessings of following Jesus, you have a faint idea of how awesome this experience will be in heaven. God would not

---

[58] (gotquestions.org)

take away something so good if He did not replace it with something better. We will surely look at every person in heaven as a precious soul that joins together for joy and praises to our God.

Can you imagine being like an angel in heaven whose physical form is like the resurrected body of Jesus? He was able to appear or disappear. Walls of confinement were not an issue for angels or for Jesus. They appeared where they wanted and left when they so desired. We will be like that.

Where Will We Be?

The next question is **where will we be?** The question immediately brings me to the truth recorded in Acts 1:11. Two men in white apparel appeared to the disciples,

"Which also said, Ye men of Galilee, why stand ye gazing up into heaven? This same Jesus, which is taken up from you into heaven, shall so come in like manner as ye have seen him go into heaven."

The idea of heaven has an upward connotation. But when you consider up at the North Pole and up at the South Pole, we are talking opposite directions. The Bible talks about three heavens. 2 Corinthians12:2 talks about the third heaven. Since there is a third heaven, there must be a first and second heaven also.

At the beginning of the Bible, we are introduced to the plurality of heavens. Genesis 1:1 says that God created *"the heavens."* There is more than one heaven, there are heavens. Throughout the Bible, they are clearly described so we can understand that there is the atmospheric heaven, the outer space, and the throne of God.

A short, well-defined presentation is given online explaining the three heavens. The first heaven is the atmosphere around the earth. In describing the rain that brought on the Flood of Noah's time, Genesis 7:11 says *"the windows of heaven were opened."* Commenting on the extent of the water, verse 19 says, *"all the high hills under the whole heaven were covered."*

The second heaven is commonly referred to as "outer space." Exodus 32:13 is one of many references to "the stars of heaven." Stars are not in the skies from which the rain falls, but in the space beyond our atmosphere. Nehemiah 9:6 also refers to space as heaven: *"You alone are the Lord; you have made heaven, the heaven of heavens, with all their host [the planets and stars]."*

A "third heaven" is mentioned in 2 Corinthians 12:1-4. Paul also called it "Paradise" in verse 4. That word is from the Greek word for park or garden—not just any park or garden, but a magnificent one. It's the same word used in the standard Greek translation of the Old Testament, the Septuagint, to mean the Garden of Eden.

Revelation 4:2 reveals that God's throne is in heaven, but which one? Obviously, God's throne is not in the sky where the clouds are and the birds fly—the first heaven. Nor is it in the visible confines of outer space—the second heaven. Putting this reference together with what Paul wrote in 2 Corinthians, we discern that the third heaven, then, must refer to the location of the throne of God.[59]

When we get to heaven, we will be in the presence of God on His throne, enjoying the best that the universe has to offer. We will have access to the earth to enjoy the new version of

---

[59] (ucg.org)

the new earth and new heaven. How can anyone fully imagine what God's place and the throne are like? I'm sure it will be wonderful.

One of the names given to the Lord Jesus is "wonderful" in Isaiah 9:6. The name "Wonderful" is interesting when we consider His Throne. Wonderful means, *"of a sort that causes or arouses wonder; amazing; astonishing."* It comes from the word wonder which means "to be filled with admiration, amazement, or awe, marvel, to think or speculate curiously." If this is His name, what will His place or His throne be like? Paul says in 1 Corinthians 2:9 *"But as it is written, Eye hath not seen, nor ear heard, neither have entered into the heart of man, the things which God hath prepared for them that love him."* We can only imagine what heaven will be like or what is awaiting all believers.

To help us understand what we will see, we will briefly consider the Holy Scriptures and try to grasp the wonder of it all. Since God's throne is beyond the stars, let's consider what we must pass to be beyond the stars.

According to "Sky and Telescope," they say it is important to distinguish between the universe as a whole and the observable universe. We can only observe objects up to a certain distance from Earth — light from more distant objects hasn't had time to reach us yet. To answer the question, "how many stars are there?" we must limit the discussion to what we can observe. Astronomers estimate that the observable universe has more than 100 billion galaxies. Our own Milky Way is home to around 300 billion stars, but it's not representative of galaxies in general. The Milky Way is a titan compared to abundant but faint dwarf galaxies, and it in turn is dwarfed by rare giant elliptical galaxies, which can be 20 times more massive. By measuring the number and luminosity of observable galaxies, astronomers put current estimates of the total stellar population at roughly 70 billion trillion (7 x 10(22).[60]

I'm sure we will be amazed, way before we get to the throne of God, even if it is in the midst of all the stars above. It is described in the book of Revelation. John, the author of the book, saw the throne in heaven. (Rev. 4:2).

Revelation 4:3 says: *"and someone was sitting on it who looked like "a jasper stone and a sardius."*

An emerald-like rainbow encircled the throne (Rev. 4:3). Lightning and thunder were emitted from the throne (Rev. 4:5).

There were twenty-four elders representing the Church seated on twenty-four thrones surrounding the main throne (Rev. 4:4). They were dressed in white and wore golden crowns (Rev. 4:4).

There were well in excess of 400 million angels surrounding the throne praising Him, who sat on the throne and the Lamb. Rev. 5:11 says: *"Then I looked, and I heard the voice of many angels around the throne, the living creatures, and the elders; and the number of them was ten thousand times ten thousand, and thousands of thousands."*

I know all of this is overwhelming and unfathomable, but it gives us an idea of what to expect.

The one part of heaven that I like to wonder about is the New Jerusalem because we are given details about it. In time, the old earth will be destroyed. New Jerusalem appears when Old Earth and Old Heavens have been destroyed (Rev. 21:1-3). The New Jerusalem, the holy city for the saints of God, comes down out of heaven. The description of this place alone

---

[60] (M. Temming)

is overwhelming, and out of this world literally. This will be part of our eternal home.

The Apostle John says in Revelation 21:10-11 *"And he carried me away in the spirit to a great and high mountain, and shewed me that great city, the holy Jerusalem, descending out of heaven from God, having the glory of God: and her light [was] like unto a stone most precious, even like a jasper stone, clear as crystal."* Without going into all the details of this place, I want to mention at least the dimensions and the materials used. John continues in Revelations 21:16 *"And the city lieth foursquare, and the length is as large as the breadth: and he measured the city with the reed, twelve thousand furlongs. The length and the breadth and the height of it are equal."* This means that the height and width and length are of equal size. The corresponding measurements are around 1500 miles wide, 1500 miles long and 1500 miles high. Since we are given the dimensions of the wall, it is evident that this city from Heaven will be inhabited between the walls. There are twelve gates to get in. We will be living inside and not on the outside surface like we do on earth. If the New Jerusalem had levels of one mile in between, we would then have 1500 levels which mean there is about 60 times more surface area in the New Jerusalem than there is on the earth.

In John 14:2 Jesus said, *"In my Father's house are many mansions: if it were not so, I would have told you. I go to prepare a place for you."* I believe Christians will have a mansion in heaven, and precisely in this city. It will be the city for the Jews and Gentiles. When our imagination takes over and we start wondering about the one who is wonderful and does wonders we are left with a feeble imagination of what we are looking at.

We are satisfied with our humble condo of one thousand square feet. But supposing our new mansion has thousands of square feet. What if every Christian had a mansion the size of the biggest known estate in the United States? The Biltmore Estate is a large private estate and tourist attraction in Asheville, North Carolina. Biltmore House, the main house on the estate, is a Châteauesque-styled mansion built by George Washington Vanderbilt II between 1889 and 1895 and is the largest privately owned house in the United States, at 178,926 square feet (16,622.8 m2) of floor space (135,280 square feet (12,568 m2) of living area). The Biltmore Mansion has 250 rooms. Still owned by one of Vanderbilt's descendants, it stands today as one of the most prominent remaining examples of the Gilded Age. In 2007, it was ranked eighth in America's Favorite Architecture by the American Institute of Architects.[61]

So, if we had a mansion with that kind of space, the New Jerusalem would have the space available for over 125 billion Biltmore Estates. Let us go a little further in our imagination. What if we had a mansion the size of the Empire state building? The New Jerusalem has enough space inside to fit roughly 9 billion Empire State buildings in the confines of its walls. God has in store for His children something so beautiful, it will take an eternity to fathom the privilege of being coinheritor with Jesus the Christ.

There are two last descriptions concerning the New Jerusalem; the colors and what it is made of.
Revelation 21:19-20 says:
[19] And the foundations of the wall of the city were garnished with all manner of precious stones. The first foundation was

---

[61] (wikipedia.org)

jasper; the second, sapphire; the third, a chalcedony; the fourth, an emerald.[20] *The fifth, sardonyx; the sixth, sardius; the seventh, chrysolyte; the eighth, beryl; the ninth, a topaz; the tenth, a chrysoprasus; the eleventh, a jacinth; the twelfth, an amethyst.*

Here is a breakdown of what substance and colors we will see.

Jasper = Diamond

Sapphire = A brilliant blue stone

Chalcedony = Sky blue with colored stripes

Emerald = Bright green stone

Sardonyx = Red and white striped stone

Sardius = Various Shades of Red

Chrysolite = Transparent gold or yellow

Beryl = Shades of green, yellow and blue

Topaz = Yellowish green

Chrysoprasus = Gold tinted green

Jacinth = Blue or violet colored

Amethyst = Purple stone

And the twelve gates were twelve pearls: every gate was made of pearl: and the street of the city was pure gold, as it were transparent glass. (Revelation 21:21)

Every gate will be one pearl, each large enough to cover the gateway to this vast city. In addition, the street of the city will be "pure gold, like unto clear glass," indicating that believers will walk on golden streets. The holy city of God will be so magnificent that believers will literally walk on precious metals that today are used for costly adornments.[62]

We have all the reasons in the universe to be looking forward to the day that God calls us home for a better life, a better place, and a better and perfect body.

---

[62] (Commentary)

Who Will We See In Heaven?

The greatest person to ever have the privilege to see is **God**. Yes, we will see God. Finally for those that knew Him and served Him on this earth, they will have an overwhelming joy to see Him face to face. From that time forward we will not live by faith but by sight. To see God is the greatest privilege this universe could allow. When we see Him it will not be on the basis that we deserve to see Him, but He, through His grace, allowed us to be in His presence. We are so insignificant compared to the universe, yet He wants us to join Him and the angels around His throne forever. Heaven will reveal the fundamental truth that we never deserved to be in His presence to start with, yet we are finally going to see Him because of grace. What overwhelming moments that will last for all of Eternity.

In Exodus chapter 33 we see Moses called to lead the Israelites to the promised land. Moses is reluctant because he is not sure since he never saw God. So, he says this....

17 And the LORD said unto Moses, I will do this thing also that thou hast spoken: for thou hast found grace in my sight, and I know thee by name.

18 And he said, I beseech thee, shew me thy glory.

19 And he said, I will make all my goodness pass before thee, and I will proclaim the name of the LORD before thee; and will be gracious to whom I will be gracious, and will shew mercy on whom I will shew mercy.

20 And he said, Thou canst not see my face: for there shall no man see me, and live.

21 And the LORD said, Behold, there is a place by me, and thou shalt stand upon a rock:

22 And it shall come to pass, while my glory passeth by, that I will put thee in a clift of the rock, and will cover thee with my hand while I pass by:

23 And I will take away mine hand, and thou shalt see my back parts: but my face shall not be seen.

When we see God, we will not be in a cleft of a rock, neither will we be covered. We shall see God in His glory, on His Throne. What a day that will be! We will see the Father, the Son, and the Holy Ghost. We will see the Trinity and we will be amazed. This reminds me of that great hymn "What a day that will be." written by Jim Hill

What a day that will be,
When my Jesus I shall see,
And I look upon His face,
The One who saved me by His grace;
When He takes me by the hand,
And leads me through the Promised Land,
What a day, glorious day that will be.

We will see Jesus and the marks of the cross on His body, the nail prints in His hands and feet and where the spear pierced His side. By faith we believe the message of the cross, but then we will see the message of the cross on His body. In 1 Timothy 6:16, God is described in terms of the reflected brilliance of precious stones. Revelation 5:6 tells us that in heaven, the Lamb stands in the center of the throne and there are descriptions of Him clothed in brilliant white. Since the Lamb represents Christ Jesus, and we know that human eyes have beheld Him after His resurrection and glorification, it seems reasonable to conclude that in heaven, we will be able to look upon our Lord and Savior.

We will see the Holy Spirit who by the very nature of His being, is able to move at will and take various forms. When Jesus was baptized, the Holy Spirit descended on Him in the form of a dove (Matthew 3:13-17). At Pentecost, the Holy Spirit was accompanied by a loud rushing noise and was seen as tongues of fire (Acts 2:1-4).[63]

I believe that we will be able to see the Holy Spirit, having a form possibly different than the way He manifested Himself on earth.

We will also see angels. There are only two angels mentioned in the Bible that refer to the ones that serve God. Other angels are mentioned, the fallen angels, and those that minister to God's children. The two well-known angels are Gabriel and the Archangel Michael.

Gabriel is the most prominent angel to appear in Scripture. Each time he is mentioned, we see him act as a messenger to impart wisdom or a special announcement from God. In the book of Daniel, Gabriel appeared to the prophet Daniel to explain some visions God gave Daniel about the end times (Daniel 8:15–27; 9:20–27).

Gabriel also appears in the New Testament. He appears to Zacharias in the temple to herald the news that his wife, Elizabeth, would give birth to John. Gabriel also approaches Mary with the announcement of the birth of Christ. Later, Joseph receives guidance in a couple visits from Gabriel. Because of the monumental importance of these history-shaping announcements, it seems that Gabriel is one of God's chief messengers.

The second angel the Bible calls by name is Michael, who functions very differently. Michael is an archangel, which

---

[63] (Trinity In Heaven?)

means "chief angel"; this title indicates that Michael holds a high rank in heaven. Although it is not certain that Michael is the only archangel, the possibility exists, according to Jude 9, where Michael is referred to definite terms as *"the* Archangel Michael." If other archangels exist, it is likely that Michael leads them.[64]

What do angels do? According to Psalm 91:11 *"For he shall give his angels charge over thee, to keep thee in all thy ways. "* Another translation uses the word "guard" from harm and danger. Ultimately God protects us, but he uses angels to keep us safe. We are not limited to one guardian angel, but possibly many. From what we gather in the Bible, angels watch and sometimes direct God's children.

The Apostle Paul said that angels were watching the apostles and they learned truths about God. After seeing the Apostles ministry, the angels were probably saying, *Wow, look how God transformed these ordinary, sinful men into apostles.* Then what did the angels do? They praised God!

I believe we will see the angels that took care of us. We will especially be interested in meeting those that have ministered to us while we were on earth.

Hebrews 1:14 says; *"Are they not all ministering spirits, sent forth to minister for them who shall be heirs of salvation?"* Angels are sent from God to minister to the children of God.

Many times the angels were sent to guide God's disciples. In heaven we will see the angels that came to our rescue and will be amazed, and awed at how many angels accompanied us throughout our lifetime. Imagine not only meeting them but

---

[64] (gotquestions.com)

hearing what they did for us. I have never had an angel appear to me and direct me to a particular place, but I wonder how many of the *coincidences* of life are actually due to an unseen angel that has stepped in and guided somebody to do something. For example, how many automobile accidents have been averted because angels have guided the drivers to safety?

Those same angels give God the glory every time they see us have victory over sin and danger. We will meet and have fellowship with them, and together give praises to God for all they did for us. To know and learn of all the incidents that required angelic intervention during our lifetime will make us kneel in adoration and praise Almighty God. Imagine listening to their testimony of how they were used by God to minister to us. It will take many years in eternity to hear and enjoy how good God was to us in every situation.

We will also see the saints of the Old and New Testament. We will meet Adam and Eve, Joseph, Moses, Noah the ark builder, David the psalmist, Solomon the preacher, Isaiah the prophet, Ezekiel, Jeremiah, Jonas, and all the saints of the New Testament like Mathew, Mark, Luke and John, John the Baptist, the apostles and the list goes on. It will be a great day as we get to know each one on a personal basis and have eternity to do so.

We will also see our loved ones that were saved. Not all relatives will be there. Only those that followed the Lord Jesus as their master will be there. We long to see our parents that lived for the Lord, and who brought us up, teaching us the Holy Scriptures. Our siblings that knew the Lord will be there. All our friends in Christ will be there. We have a strong desire to see our children and grandchildren there one day. Since there is no time in Heaven, we will all be gathered in a short span of time to spend eternity together. We know how hard it is to lose a loved one. So the moment will be significant when we see our loved ones again. We will embrace them and never be separated ever again. What a special day that will be!

What Will We Do In Heaven?

The last question we will consider is **what will we do in heaven?** For starters, we will see God and visit His throne and speak with Him. We might have talked to God in prayer all of our lives, but now we will talk to him face to face. Will we be in wonder just to hear the voice of God? If it sounds like thunder because of His grandeur, we will enjoy every moment? His voice may give us another sense of how great is our God.

We will get to know Him well, and will have sweet fellowship with Him. I don't know about you, but I have a lot of questions for Him. Maybe being in His presence will illuminate many issues. Since we will never be God and know everything, we will still have to learn. I hope that in our curiosity, we will be able to ask any question we want. We will have all eternity to have our questions answered.

I also believe we will enjoy sounds in heaven. We know there are trumpets and harps.

Revelation 14:2 says, *"And I heard a voice from heaven, as the voice of many waters, and as the voice of a great thunder: and I heard the voice of harpers harping with their harps."* We now know that Lucifer is a fallen angel. His origin was in heaven and Ezekiel 28:13 tells us that at his creation was a minister of music, with tabrets and pipes. Though he is no longer there, music continues in the heavenly realm. Music can be calming or invigorating, and stimulating. Man has done an excellent job in some music presentations, but nothing compared to the One that created it. Imagine listening to every sound in heaven, and the beautiful harmonious melody of God's love for us.

Since the Word of God is eternal, I can speculate that we will know it much better than we know it today. We will have the preacher of preachers explain what He said and what He meant. It will take an eternity to hear every word revealed in such understanding ways. The Psalmist said in Psalms 119:120, *"How sweet are thy words unto my taste! yea, sweeter than honey to my mouth!."*

Matthew 4:4 says, *"But he answered and said, It is written, Man shall not live by bread alone, but by every word that proceedeth out of the mouth of God."*

1 Peter 1:25 says *"But the word of the Lord endureth forever."* Isaiah 40:8 *"The grass withereth, the flower fadeth: but the word of our God shall stand for ever."*

Since the Bible is eternal, we will be taught the eternal truths. We will have no human infirmities to hinder comprehension and a memory capacity that will be useful throughout eternity.

We will have time to visit the new heavens and the new earth, and fellowship with all the saints in heaven. If all the Christians and angels take time to give their testimony of what God did for them on the earth prior to heaven, we will know each other very well and appreciate how God manifested His grace in so many ways. We will need eternity to hear everyone and give God glory.

We will drink the purest and most refreshing water, the universe has to offer. Revelation 22:1 says, *And he shewed me a pure river of water of life, clear as crystal, proceeding out of the throne of God and of the Lamb.* A commentator says; The heavenly state which was before described as a city, and called the new Jerusalem, is here described as a paradise, alluding to the earthly paradise which was lost by the sin of the first Adam; here is another paradise restored by the second Adam. A paradise in a city, or a whole city in a paradise! In the first paradise, there were only two persons to behold the beauty and taste the pleasures of it, but in this second paradise whole cities and nations shall find abundant delight and satisfaction. And here observe the river of paradise. The earthly paradise was well watered: no place can be pleasant or fruitful that is not so. This river is described, by its fountain-head—*the throne of God and the Lamb.* All our springs of grace, comfort, and glory are in God, and all our streams from him are through the mediation of the Lamb. Its quality is, *pure and clear as crystal.* All the streams of earthly comfort are muddy, but these are clear, salutary, and refreshing, giving life and preserving life, to those who drink of them.[65]

We will also eat in heaven. Not that we have to, but for the pleasure of eating. Enjoying good food will be one beautiful pleasure of paradise. If you enjoy fruit now, you will be introduced to the ultimate taste of fruit. John the author of Revelation says in 22:2, *In the midst of the street of it, and on either side of the river, was there the tree of life, which bare twelve manner of fruits, and yielded her fruit every month: and the leaves of the tree were for the healing of the nations.*

Notice that the tree of life was on both sides of the river on both banks of the river coming from the throne of God in the new city prepared for us. Can you imagine this beautiful scene?

Barnes' Notes on the Bible points out that in the street or streets of the city, as well as on the banks of the river, the tree

---

[65] (Tools)

of life was planted. It abounded everywhere. The city had not only a river passing through it, but streets pervaded it, and all those streets were lined and shaded by this tree. The idea in the mind of the writer is that of Eden or Paradise, but it is not the Eden of the book of Genesis, or the Oriental or Persian Paradise: it is a picture where all is combined, that in the view of the writer would constitute beauty, or contribute to happiness.[66]

Let us not forget that if the river ran from just one side of the city to the other side it would be 1500 miles long. So wherever we are there will be streets and trees with clear water and we will enjoy food forever. Every month the tree will produce twelve kinds of fruit on the same tree.

We will have a marvelous celebration for joining Jesus in heaven called the "the marriage supper of the lamb." All Christians will most likely sit at the table and have the greatest feast ever.

As one author put it, the Marriage Supper of the Lamb will be a wrap-up party like no other. It will be a victory celebration as well as a marriage feast. Both celebrations will be combined into one. The whole event will be an introduction to the eternal realms of God. It will be a consummation and serendipity of unspeakable glory.

The apostle Peter tells us that the angels desire to look into these wonders. They are very interested in what God intends to do in and through His saints. (1Pet.1:12) Clearly, these matters are beyond our understanding right now. They are just too wonderful for our present comprehension.[67]

---

[66] (B. N. Bible)
[67] (Pilgrim)

I believe that God will introduce us to His creation. We will probably visit every planet, every star, galaxy, and the universe and learn about their distinct differences with each other. I have a feeling that we will be able to travel from one place to another without wings or mobile devices. Just like Jesus, all of a sudden, appeared to the disciples in a closed and locked room. We will probably have the opportunity of studying every layer of every planet, and its composition and origin. We will be amazed at God's creative plan that He had as He was thinking of sharing it with his people who through faith become co-inheritors with Christ.

We cannot even begin to imagine what God has in store for us for eternity. It will be marvelous, impressive, inspiring, ful-filling, satisfying, gratifying, breathtaking, heart-wrenching, beautiful, fantastic, a place for perfect happiness and fun. All those that believed and are saved will be there. We hope to meet you there, as you journey to the end. May you find **hope through cancer**.

Notes and Thoughts On, "The Bridge."

Works Cited

Adams, Lisa. *The stupid things people say to those with cancer &
their families.* Feb 2013.
http://lisabadams.com/2013/02/27/the-stupid-things-
people-say-to-people-with-cancertheir-families/.

America, Cancer Treatment Centers Of. "About Your Cancer, the
financial stress of cancer treatment." n.d. 2014
http://www.cancercenter.com/discussions/blog/managing
-the-financial-stress-of-cancer-treatment/).

Author, unknown. "inspirational Spark." n.d.
http;//www.inspirationalspark.com.

Baertlein, Lisa. *Chemotherapy and Your Immune System.* n.d.
everydayhealth.com.

Bell, Caleb K. *Religion News Service.* RNS, n.d.
http://www.religionnews.com/2013/04/04/poll-
americans-love-the-bible-but-dont-read-it-much/.

Bible, Barnes Notes On The. *Revelation 22:2.* n.d.
http://biblehub.com/commentaries/revelation/22-2.htm .

Bible, King James Version Of The. *King James Version Of The Bible.*
1 John 4:10, n.d.

Bible.org. "Psalm 23." (n.d.). https://bible.org/article/exposition-
psalm-23 .

—. "Psalm 23." (n.d.). https://bible.org/article/exposition-psalm-23
.

Board, Cancer.Net Editorial. *Maintenance Chemotherapy.* n.d.
http://www.cancer.net/navigating-cancer-care/how-

cancer-treated/chemotherapy/maintenance-
chemotherapy).

Brown, H. Jackson. n.d.
http://www.brainyquote.com/quotes/keywords/remembe
r.html#KLjGXzBE4AVo38Ai.99.

Bruce, Sandy. *The Wild Branches.* n.d.
http://thewildolivebranches.blogspot.com/2012/03/valley-
of-shadow-of-death-by-sandy.html .

Care, Cancer. "Understanding and Managing Chemotherapy Side
Effects." n.d. http://www.cancercare.org/publications.

Casper, Cindy. *First Response.* Our Daily Bread, 2014.
http://odb.org/2014/10/25/first-response/comment-page-
1/?s=prayer#comments .

Cassidy, Susan. *Finances.* n.d.
http://money.howstuffworks.com/personal-
finance/financial-planning/10-reasons-to-start-a-
trust.htm#page=0.

—. *Finances.* n.d. http://money.howstuffworks.com/personal-
finance/financial-planning/10-reasons-to-start-a-
trust.htm#page=0.

Center., Venderbilt-Ingram Cancer. "Self Image And Self Esteem
Concerns." n.d.
http://www.vicc.org/cancercare/symptoms/counseling/im
age.php.

Chardon, Dominique. "Helping Hobbies That Built Self Esteem." *Self
Esteem By Girl And Talk* (2013). http://dr-
carol.com/2013/02/01/helping-hobbies-that-build-self-

esteem-when-you-help-others-you-sometimes-help-yourself/.

CNBCnews. 2006. http://www.cbsnews.com/news/cancer-patients-more-than-twice-as-likely-to-go-bankrupt-study-shows/.

CNN. "Couples Living With Cancer," n.d. cnn http://www.cnn.com/2011/LIVING/07/21/sick.couples.o/.

commentary. *The New Jerusalem*. n.d. http://www.discoverrevelation.com/Rev_21.html.

Commentary. *The New Jerusalem*. n.d. http://www.discoverrevelation.com/Rev_21.html.

Commentary, Barnes. n.d.

Commentary, Clarks. *The Shepherd*. Godvine.com, n.d. http://www.godvine.com/bible/psalms/23-.

Commerford, Brianna. "Stories of Hope." n.d. http://www.cancer.org/treatment/survivorshipduringanda ftertreatment/storiesofhope/childhood-cancer-survivor-finds-her-voice.

Dehaan, Dennis J. *Playing God*. Our Dail Bread, 1994. http://odb.org/1994/03/05/playing-god/.

E.W.Bullinger. *Number 7 In Scripture*. 1952. The Lamp Press, London,

Encyclopedia, Wikipedia. *Palm Branch (symbol)*. n.d. http://en.wikipedia.org/wiki/Palm_branch_(symbol)_trunc ated.

Felicetti, Marcus Julian. *10 Healing Benefits Of The Sun*. 2012.
    http://www.mindbodygreen.com .

Fisher, Dennis. *The Hand Of God*. 2015.
    http://odb.org/2015/01/27/the-hand-of-god/.

Gaffney, Patricia. *The Saving Graces*. n.d.
    http://www.goodreads.com/work/quotes/126092-the-
    saving-graces.

gotquestions.com. *Michael the Archangel*. n.d.
    http://www.gotquestions.org/names-of-
    angels.html#ixzz3SOG1cfiF.

gotquestions.org. n.d. http://www.gotquestions.org/look-like-in-
    Heaven.html#ixzz3RwyBXWrk .

—. *Trinity In Heaven?* n.d. http://www.gotquestions.org/see-
    Trinity-heaven.html#ixzz3SJmdGjQk.

Henry, Matthew. *Confidence in God's grace and care*. Matthew
    Henry's Concise Commentary, n.d.
    http://www.christnotes.org/commentary.php?com=mhc&
    b=19&c=23.

Hoggart, Michael. *The Number 7, God's Divine Number*. n.d.
    http://www.fillthevoid.org/Apologetics/number7MikeHogg
    ard.html .

Hausmann, Michael. *Is The Bible Truly God's Word*. n.d.
    www.gotquestions.org.

http://en.wikipedia.org/wiki/Shepherd. *The Good Shepherd*.
    Wikipedia, the free encyclopedia, n.d.

Keller, Phillip. *A Shepherd Looks At Psalm 23*. 2014.
    http://www.antipas.org/commentaries/articles/shepherd_
    psa23/shepherd_07.html.

Kercheville, Brent. (2005).
    http://www.christianmonthlystandard.com/index.php/the-
    brevity-of-life/.

M.R.Dehaan. "Living O rJust Alive." April25,2001.
    http://odb.org/2001/04/25/living-or-just-alive/ .

McCasland, David. Our Daily Bread, n.d.
    http://odb.org/2015/01/29/our-source-of-help/ .

Merill, Mark. "10 Ways T Be Remembered a 100 years from now."
    n.d. http://www.allprodad.com/.

Nakazawa, Donna Jackson. "How A Marriage Survives When One
    Partner Gets Sick." n.d.
    http://www.more.com/relationships/marriage-
    divorce/how-marriage-survives-when-one-partner-gets-
    sick?page=2.

Nolo. *Nolo's Guide To Living Trust*. n.d.
    http://nolonow.nolo.com/noe/popup/living_trust_guide.p
    df.

Pilgrim, End Time. *The Marriage Supper Of The Lamb*. n.d.
    http://endtimepilgrim.org/marriage.htm.

Proflowers. "Primary Significance: Love and Romance." *History and
    Meaning Behind Red Roses*. 2012.
    http://www.proflowers.com/blog/history-and-meaning-
    behind-red-roses.

Radwan, Farouk. *Lack of enthusiasm and depression*. n.d.
http://www.2knowmyself.com/depression/Lack_of_enthus
iasm_and_depression.

Roper, David. *Travelling Companion*. Our Daily Bread, 2013. .
http://odb.org/2013/11/19/traveling-companion/.

Services, U.S.Department For Health & Human. "Life After Cancer."
Facing Forward. n.d.
http://www.cancer.gov/publications/patient-
education/life-after-treatment.pdf .

Siebert, Al. "Deep Survival." *Who Lives, Who Dies, And Why* n.d.

Society, American Cancer. *Chemo Brain* n.d.
http://www.cancer.org/treatment/treatmentsandsideeffec
ts/physicalsideeffects/chemotherapyeffects/chemo-brain.

—. *Dealing With A Parents Terminal Illness*. n.d.
http://www.cancer.org/treatment/childrenandcancer/help
ingchildrenwhenafamilymemberhascancer/dealingwithapa
rentsterminalillness/dealing-with-a-parents-terminal-
illness-intro .

—. "Support Groups, What is the evidence?" n.d.
http://www.cancer.org.

Spiegel, D. *Minding the body:Psychotherapy and cancer survival*.
2013.

Spurgeon, Charles. *The Peace Of God*. 1878. ,
http://www.spurgeongems.org/vols22-24/chs1397.pdf.

—. *The Peace Of God*. 1872.
http://www.spurgeongems.org/vols22-24/chs1397.pdf .

—. "The Treasury Of David." (n.d.).
http://www.spurgeon.org/treasury/ps023.

Tada, Joni Eareckson. *A place of Healing*. n.d. Wrestling with the
mysteries of suffering.

Temming, Maria. *How many stars are there in the universe?* 2014.
http://www.skyandtelescope.com/astronomy-
resources/how-many-stars-are-
there/#sthash.CnQCif0E.dpuf.

"The Importance Of Hobbies And Stress Relief." 2014.
http://www.coreproducts.com/blog/2014/05/06/the-
importance-of-hobbies-for-happiness-and-stress-relief/.

Tools, Bible Study. *Revelation 22:1*. n.d.
http://www.biblestudytools.com/commentaries/matthew-
henry-complete/revelation/22.html.

Trinity In Heaven? n.d. http://www.gotquestions.org/see-Trinity-
heaven.html#ixzz3SJmdGjQk.

ucg.org. *What does the Bible mean by the "third heaven"*. n.d.
http://www.ucg.org/bible-faq/what-does-bible-mean-
third-heaven.

University, Perdue. "Center for the study of religion & American
Culture." n.d. http://www.raac.iupui.edu/about/.

Vander-Lugt, Herbert. *How Is Your Vision*. 1999.
http://odb.org/1999/02/20/how-is-your-vision/.

Wellman, Jack. *What does the Bible say Heaven is like?* 2011.
http://www.whatchristianswanttoknow.com/what-does-
the-bible-say-heaven-is-like/#ixzz3RMYMePFf.

White, Ellen G. *God's Love For Man*. n.d.
      http://www.whiteestate.org/books/sc/sc1.html.

Whitelocks, Sadie. *Cancer survivors suffer psychological scars* .
      2011. Dailymail.com.

Wikipedia. The free Encyclopedia, n.d. http://en.wikipedia.org/.

Wikipedia. "Chemoreceptor trigger zone." n.d.
      http://en.wikipedia.org/wiki/Chemoreceptor_trigger_zone.

wikipedia.org. *The Biltmore Estste*. n.d.
      http://en.wikipedia.org/wiki/Biltmore_Estate .

About the Authors

Faith Copeland Jacques:
Born in Pennsylvania and 42 year resident of Florida.
Wife and mother of three children and has five grandchildren.
A licensed practical nurse, and worked 15 years in the medical field.
A licensed Esthetician and Massage Therapist.
Co-founder of "Hope Through Cancer" ministry.

Claude Jacques:
Father of three sons and has five grandchildren.
Ordained Baptist Minister and Pastor for 25 years.
Founder of the French Baptist Church in Thetford Mines, Quebec, Canada.
Fifteen years in the radio ministry.
Wrote more than 3,000 sermons in French.
Taught Church History and Homiletics at the Lennoxville Bible College in Lennoxville, Quebec, Canada.
Founder of "Hope Through Cancer" ministry.
Artist.

Toni Williams
Assistant Editor

Toni attended Penn Hall College majoring in English, has two married sons and six precious grandchildren. She has her private pilot's license and enjoyed flying for many years with her pilot husband. After her recovery, she became active in Cancer Care, "a Christ-centered fellowship for those suffering with cancer or caring for someone stricken by this disease." She knows experientially that God can make "beauty from ashes" and has a purpose for all suffering. She comes alongside those going through cancer to pray with them, cry, laugh, encourage, share information, call, visit, email, and accompany them to medical appointments. As a "survivor and thriver" she enjoys walking, swimming, a good laugh, and being involved at her church at Calvary Chapel in Fort Lauderdale, Florida, where her gift of hospitality frequently finds her guest room filled with visiting friends or those in need of care.